BOOTS & SEX ED

UGLY STICK SALOON BOOK #2

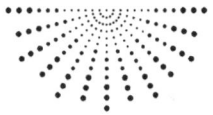

MYLA JACKSON

ELLE JAMES

TWISTED PAGE INC

BOOTS & SEX ED

UGLY STICK SALOON SERIES BOOK #2

New York Times & USA Today
Bestselling Author

ELLE JAMES

writing as

MYLA JACKSON

EBOOK ISBN: 978-1-62695-102-0

PRINT ISBN: 978-1-62695-103-7

❧ Created with Vellum

*This book is dedicated people who know what they want
and go after it until they finally succeed.*

Sex Ed...Cowboy Style

Kendall has loved sexy cowboy Ed Johnson since the first time she saw him taming wild horses. Now Kendall is twenty-one, legal and ready to be more than friends. In her bid to win his affections she asks Ed to give her a few Sex Education lessons about what makes a cowboy hot.

Ed promised Kendall's brother he'd keep an eye on his little sister while he's away defending their country. But Ed's pretty darn certain Sex Education lessons aren't what big brother had in mind. Caught between his pledge and a recently matured little sex kitten, Ed struggles to keep his word, while giving Kendall what she wants, Sex Ed.

Warning: *Determined young woman, unsuspecting cowboy and a feisty roommate add up to fun lessons on how to make a cowboy hot.*

AUTHOR'S NOTE

Enjoy other Ugly Stick Saloon books by Myla
Jackson
Ugly Stick Saloon Series
Boots & Chaps (#1)
Boots & Sex Ed (#2)
Boots & Leather (#3)
Boots & Promises (#4)
Boots & Bareback (#5)
Boots & Dirty Tricks (#6)
Boots & Lace (#7)
Boots & Roses (#8)
Boots & Buckles (#9)
Boots & the Wishes (#10)
Boots & Twisters (#11)
Boots & the Bachelor (#12)
Boots & The Rogue (#13)
Boots & The Heartbreaker (#14)
Boots & Wings (#15)

Visit Mylajackson.com for more information
Visit her alter ego Elle James at ellejames.com
Join Elle James and Myla Jackson's Newsletter at
http://ellejames.com/ElleContact.htm

*E*dward Judson slapped his dusty cowboy hat against his leg as he led his black gelding into the barn. The sun baked the weathered boards of the exterior, while the interior remained relatively cool. It took a few moments for his eyes to adjust to the shadows. "I traded that stock yesterday, made enough to pay off my land and put a hefty chunk of cash down on a house."

"Good move." Grant Fowler slung a leg over the pinto mare and dropped to the ground.

Ed owed Grant a lot for teaching him everything he knew about trading shares on the stock market. The man owned a 5,000-acre ranch for a reason. Not because he was good at raising horses, but because he was damned good at managing money.

"You don't need my advice anymore, Ed," Grant said. "You could go into financial planning yourself with a few courses for certification."

"Not interested." Ed had just begun to understand the stock market's full potential and seeing the fruits of his trades pay off. But he didn't need a lot of money, just enough for his own purposes.

"You gonna work training horses for other people like me the rest of your life?"

"Nope." Ed grinned. "Not that I don't appreciate the work and all, but I got plans of my own."

"Whatcha gonna do with two hundred acres, Ed?"

"Get married someday, settle down, raise a family and some horses. It's what I'm good at." He shifted his boots in the loose dirt of the barn floor. "The horses part."

"You're good at day-trading, dude."

"I'll do that on the side so that I can afford my horses too."

Grant shook his head, a smile spreading across his face. "Okay, I get it. Can't say that I blame you. At least when you're trading for yourself, you don't have the responsibility of other people's money hanging over you."

"You hit the nail on the head."

"So how is babysitting Connor Mason's sister? Saw her at the Ugly Stick Saloon last night." Grant whistled. "Looks to me like you got yourself a hot little handful in that one."

Ed's muscles tightened, his pulse kicking up a notch as he stepped around the end of the stall. "What do you mean?"

Grant held up his hands. "Nothing, buddy. Not a thing. Just that she's a pretty girl."

"Yeah and every man in the building was drooling over her. I get it. Don't add to the crowd, will ya?" He should never have offered to look out for Kendall Mason. Especially now that she was over twenty-one and legal in every way. As far as Ed was concerned, her body should be considered a class-one felony.

Every time he looked at her, he wanted to commit all kinds of lewd and lascivious acts. With two hard pulls, he yanked the leather strap from the girth around the horse's belly and let it fall, swinging to the other side.

Grant leaned on his saddle, apparently in no hurry whatsoever to groom his own horse or end the current conversation. "I don't see how you do it."

"Do what?" As far as Ed was concerned, Grant talked too much. If he wasn't the boss, he'd probably tell him so. Hell, he might anyway.

"I don't know how you can keep your hands off her."

For the past six months, Ed had been fighting that very urge. "Grant, you talk too much." His hands ached to get hold of Kendall and touch her in ways that had nothing to do with brotherly love.

Grant laughed out loud, then continued to rub it in.

Much to Ed's agony.

"With that body and those boobs, the temptation would kill me."

"Resist, or I might just have to kill you. And I'd hate to lose my job because I killed the boss." Ed tossed the saddle onto a nearby saddle rack and grabbed a brush from the shelf, eager to get the task done and get home.

When Grant made no move to remove his horse's saddle, it was all Ed could do not to throw the brush at the man. With quick, calming strokes, Ed curried his gelding, refusing to respond to any other conversation from Grant.

"Okay, okay, I get the hint." Grant finally turned toward his saddle and removed the strap around the horse's belly. "I'm just saying you're a better man than I am."

Ed snorted. As he ran the brush over the horse's hindquarters, his cell phone vibrated his back pocket. He pulled it out and clicked the talk button. "Yeah."

"Ed?"

Every red blood cell leaped to attention at the sound of Kendall's voice. Then they all sped south to pool in his groin. Grant had it right. Keeping his hands off Kendall was only half his problem. Keeping his mind off her had become an impossibility.

"What do you need Kendall?"

"When are you coming home? I have a project I need your help on."

"I'm not much good with school projects. Get one of your classmates to help you out."

"I would, but I'd rather you help me on this one. It's special and you're my best choice," her breath whooshed out slowly before she continued, "the only man I trust."

Ed sucked in a deep breath, his imagination running rampant over the close quarters they'd be working in. He couldn't do it. No way. *Just tell her.* "I'll be home in fifteen minutes."

"Oh, good. I'll be waiting," she whispered into his ear, and the phone went silent.

Ed had a good start on a full-blown erection by the time he climbed into his truck and turned it toward Temptation, Texas, the little backwater town he'd been born and raised in.

The short ride home from the Rockin' G Ranch wasn't nearly long enough to cool the heat building in his loins. Tomorrow, he'd start looking for a different place to live. He'd planned on living in the apartment below Kendall's until he had his own house built, but the way things were going, the way he felt about his best friend's little sister...He couldn't last much longer without doing something stupid.

As he turned onto the street where the old Ross house stood, a convertible backed out of the driveway he shared with the other two occupants. A muscular, bare-chested young man smiled and waved as he passed by with the top down, his long, bright blond hair blowing in the breeze.

His fingers tightened on the steering wheel and a frown settled between Ed's brows. Who the hell was that leaving the house he shared with Kendall and Lacey? Better be one of Lacey's conquests. She was old enough to manage her own affairs. Kendall, on the other hand, had barely been twenty-one for a few weeks. She'd better not be messing around on Ed's watch.

As he shifted into park, he glanced up at the window to Kendall's apartment. The blinds were open and Kendall stood with her side to the window, wearing nothing but a thin, lace bra and thong panties. She turned her back to the window and unclipped the bra, letting it fall down over her arms to the floor.

She might as well be naked—the thin strap of the thong cutting a line between her butt cheeks hid nothing.

Ed moaned, his cock twitched, and blood rushed in to make it swell behind his zipper. He forced anger to follow the powerful rush of lust. Did the girl have so little sense as to leave her window wide open so that any peeping Tom could look in?

With the storm of lust and righteous anger driving him forward, Ed leaped out of the car, passed the door to his apartment on the first floor and took the steps two at a time to the upper apartment where Kendall lived. He hammered on the door until Kendall flung it open.

"Oh, Ed." She cupped her hands over her naked breasts, like that did anything to hide their beautiful, lush fullness from Ed's vision. "Where's the fire?"

Ed pushed past her and marched to the window on the other side of the apartment, yanking the string on the shade so hard, the shade popped out of its slot and clattered to the floor.

Kendall giggled behind him, her eyes going wide when Ed glared.

He gathered the shade from the floor, fit the ends into the slot and lowered it with more precision and care this time. When he was done, he faced Kendall, and breathed a sigh to find her clutching a shirt to her chest. "Don't undress in front of the window. I thought your mother taught you better than that."

"There's not anyone on this street who'd care but Old Man Frantzen." She tossed her hair. "I'm sure he's so blind he couldn't see that far anyway."

Ed jerked his thumb toward the window. "You never know what perverts are lurking out there looking for an eyeful. And honey, you were giving an eyeful and then some."

Her eyelids closed to half-mast and she sidled close. "Perverts? Hum…sounds interesting." Slim fingers climbed up his chest and the shirt she held slipped lower, letting one perky nipple peek through.

Ed reached out and lifted the shirt to cover her flesh, realizing his mistake as soon as the backs of his fingers brushed over her naked skin. Stifling a groan, he jumped back. "Just close the blinds before you strip, will ya?"

"Yes, sir!" Kendall popped a salute.

That pesky shirt slipped down again to expose the other pretty breast.

A moan escaped Ed's throat and he dove for the door.

Kendall stood at her door as Ed beat a hasty retreat down the steps to his apartment. No sooner had his door slammed than Lacey's door opened across the hall from Kendall.

"Well?" Lacey pushed Kendall into her apartment and closed the door behind her. "How'd it go?"

"I don't know." Kendall frowned. "He came in all angry and left like a cat with his tail on fire."

Lacey's face split in a grin. "Did you show him some boobs?"

Heat flooded Kendall's cheeks. She held her tank top in front of her like she had positioned it for Ed. "I did this side first." She switched to let the other side be exposed. "I did this side and when he answered the door, all I had was this." She dropped the shirt altogether and covered her breasts with her hands.

"Did he touch them?"

"Yes, and no." Kendall's chest rose and fell on a heartfelt sigh. "Only to cover them."

"Did he mention Cory leaving with his shirt off?"

"Not a word." Kendal dropped onto the sofa. "What am I doing wrong?"

Lacey laughed out loud. "Honey, you did it all right."

"Then why isn't he taking the hint?"

"Oh, he took it all right. I'll bet he's taking a really cold shower right now. Shh. Listen." Lacey cupped her fingers around her ear, a smile curling the corners of her lips. "Yup, he's in the shower." She clapped her hands together. "Now, as soon as the water shuts off, be at his door ready to launch Plan B."

"I don't know. He didn't seem too excited by the idea of me being naked."

"Of course, he isn't excited by the idea of you getting naked with anyone else. I take it he closed the blinds based on the noise I heard a minute ago?" She stood with her arms crossed.

"Yeah, so?" Kendall shrugged. "My brother would have done the same. Face it, the man has a brother complex. He can't touch me because he thinks of me as his kid sister."

"Then your job is to show him you're neither his sister, nor a kid."

The pipes clanked in the wall beside Kendall, indicating the shower had been turned off below. Kendall dragged in a deep breath and let it slowly in an attempt to slow her pulse. It didn't work.

Lacey's mouth set in a firm line. "That's your cue." She herded Kendall to the door, grabbing the tank top from the floor. "Don't be too obvious too fast, it tends to scare men off. Remember Plan B. Make him think you're after someone else. Make him jealous enough to cross the brother line. Trust me, there will be no returning."

Lacey practically shoved her down the stairs.

Halfway down, Kendall got cold feet. Really cold feet. Okay, so the cool wood against her bare feet felt good compared to the heat rising up her neck into her face. She couldn't do this. She'd never been this forward in her entire life, always playing the good girl, refusing to give her brother any trouble after he'd taken on the huge responsibility of raising her when their parents had died in a car crash. Having just graduated high school, he'd barely been able to tie his own shoelaces and he'd never tied hers.

But Connor learned and attended the small college in town while showing up at all of her school events, shuttling her to and from soccer practice like any other soccer mom. He'd grown up before he'd had a chance to be a kid.

Kendall made life as easy on him as possible. She understood the sacrifice he'd made by giving up a scholarship to the University of Texas to stay home and care for his kid sister.

As soon as she graduated and was safely accepted to the local college, he'd gotten his commission into the U.S. Army and left Temptation, Texas. He'd only agreed to go on the condition his best friend would look out for his little sister.

Therein lay the problem. Some of the reasons for which Kendall had fallen in love with Ed were the same reasons he wouldn't look at her as other than Connor's little sister. He was loyal to his friends, protective to a fault, and he kept his word no matter what. And four years later, he was no different. Connor had managed to miss being deployed for the first three of Kendall's college years, but now he was deployed and Kendall was about to graduate. If she was going to get Ed to notice her, it had to be soon.

She'd hoped when she turned twenty-one, Ed would start seeing her as a grown woman, not a kid sister. Two months had passed since her birthday and nothing had changed. After a come-to-Temptation meeting with her best friend, Lacey, she'd made the decision to take matters into her own hands and push the issue.

Thus Plan A of Operation Sex Ed. *Let him see what he's missing.*

Kendall still wasn't all that sure that standing practically naked in the window had done the trick. Ed had reacted just like Ed always reacted, all protective and big-brotherly.

Enter Plan B.

Kendall stood in front of Ed's door, her hand poised over the wood. "I can't do this."

From above, Lacey called out, "Yes. You. Can."

Kendall jumped and knocked on the door before she could change her mind. As she waited for Ed to answer, she realized she was still naked and carrying the tank top. Her heart palpitated as she shoved her arms through the shirt. She'd just pulled it down over her breasts when Ed jerked open the door.

He wore nothing but a towel wrapped around his middle, his hair and body dripping from his recent shower.

Desire slammed into her belly, spreading like wildfire, frying every brain cell to a crisp. For a moment, she couldn't remember why she'd come down the stairs, then Lacey's words echoed in her head. *Remember Plan B.* Smoothing the panic out of her face and voice, she smiled up at him. "Got a minute?" Without waiting for a response, she waltzed past him, inhaling the fresh scent of soap and Ed. As she sidled by, she swung her hips in such a manner as to invite just about any hot-blooded male to rutting season with a grown woman, not a little girl. She'd purposely not pulled her shirt over her rear, leaving her naked ass exposed to his view. The thong between her butt cheeks didn't count for anything.

"Got any clothes?" Ed asked, searching the hallway before he closed the door, turned and leaned on it. "Please tell me you don't run around like that in front of the kid that left as I was getting home?"

"Cory?" She faced Ed, twisting the hem of her tank top, drawing it up enough Ed could see the triangle of black lace that was the bulk of material in the thong panties. "He likes it when I dress like this." She stood straighter, her unbound breasts naturally jutting forward. "I didn't come to talk about Cory, I came to ask for your help."

"My help?" Ed glanced down at his towel. "Could it wait until I'm dressed?"

Kendall shrugged, her lips twisting in a teasing smile. "Dressed or undressed doesn't matter to me. I need lessons, and I can't think of anyone that I trust as much as I trust you to teach me."

"Exactly what kind of lessons did you have in

mind?" Ed pushed away from the door and strode through the living room to the bedroom.

Kendall had to resist the urge to grab the towel and yank it loose. Her blood raced through her veins, molten hot for the man, and he wasn't aware she existed as anything other than Connor's sister. Why was fate so cruel?

She followed him, standing in the doorway of his bedroom, imagining lying naked in his bed, making mad passionate love. An ache built in her core, fortifying her determination to make Operation Sex Ed work.

Ed reached into his closet for a pair of jeans.

Kendall launched Plan B. "I need lessons on how to attract a man."

He spun to face her, dropping the jeans to the floor. His towel slipped and he barely caught it before it ended up with the jeans around his ankles. "What?"

Her gaze swept over his thick thighs and narrow hips, her pulse pounding in the vein at the base of her throat. "I want lessons on how to attract a man," she repeated more slowly, as if speaking to someone with limited faculties.

"I heard what you said, but what are you talking about?" He clutched his towel in front of him, the effect displaying a significant amount of leg, thigh, hips and groin.

Kendall licked her lips, her gaze fixed on the position still covered by the towel, willing Ed to expose even more. Her pussy creamed at the mere thought of seeing his cock. How would it be to hold it in her hands? Kendall's breath caught in her throat. In an attempt to concentrate, she pulled her glance up to his face. "I think I'm in love with a guy, but he doesn't have a clue I exist. I want you to help me attract his attention."

"Aren't you a little young for playing games with guys?"

"I'm not seventeen anymore, in case you hadn't noticed, and these," she pointed to her breasts, the nipples puckering on cue through the thin material of the tank top, "aren't getting any action. I need help."

Ed ran a hand through his hair, his gaze glancing off her breasts and hitting every corner of the room without looking back. "Tell me you didn't just say your...your...oh, hell, aren't getting any action."

"Boobs?" She raised her brows and stared at him. "I'm all grown up, Mr. Judson, not the little girl that used to follow you and Connor around."

"I know you're all grown up, but—"

"I'm twenty-one, single and almost finished with college." She jammed her hands onto her hips. "I deserve a sex-life just like anyone else. If you aren't going to help me figure this out, I'll find someone who will."

"Whoa, wait a minute." Ed held up his hands. "Just exactly what is it you want me to teach you? Not that I'm agreeing to this lunacy."

"I want you to show me what turns on a guy. Kind of like a sex education class for dummies. Only I'm not planning on practicing the abstinence part." Her hands skimmed over her breasts, curving down over her hips. "I want the full-blown, how-to-make-him-hot-for-me lessons."

"Holy Hell, you're kidding, right?"

"Do I look like I'm kidding?" She tapped a bare foot, realizing it probably wasn't making a big impression with her bright pink toenail polish. "Not only am I not kidding, I want lessons to begin tonight. And in payment for lessons, the pizza is on me."

"Pizza?"

The knock on the door couldn't have been timed better.

"Right on time." She smiled and fished the twenty-dollar bill out of the triangle of her panties. "I'll be right back. Don't go anywhere, we have work to do."

"Pizza?" Ed stood for a moment as though rooted to the floor, his hand still clutching the towel around his middle, his face pale, probably in shock.

Good. Kendall turned toward the door and called out, "Coming!"

She hadn't taken two steps when Ed caught up with her, ripped the twenty from her fingers and shoved her back in the bedroom. "Stay," he commanded.

Then, wearing nothing but the towel and carrying

the twenty, he opened the door to the apartment for Jason, the pizza delivery boy.

"Nice towel." Jason shoved the pizza box at Ed.

For a moment, Ed fumbled with the towel, the twenty and the pizza box.

Kendall fought back the urge to giggle, silently praying he'd slip and drop the towel.

Sadly, Ed managed to pay for the pizza and close the door behind Jason, towel intact around his middle.

Kendall came out into the living room, crossed her arms beneath her chest, giving them a little added lift. "So what's it to be? Will you teach me everything you know about making love, or do I take my pizza elsewhere?"

CHAPTER TWO

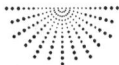

*E*d's cock twitched, tenting the terrycloth draped around his middle. He felt like an idiot, dressed in a towel, holding a pizza and answering a dynamite-loaded question from the little girl whom he'd promised to protect from lecherous males.

Only Kendall wasn't a little girl anymore and she wanted his help to seduce a man. His tongue wouldn't work, he couldn't find the words needed to talk her out of her cockamamie plan. Instead, he nodded. "Let's have pizza and talk about it."

"First, your promise." She threw her shoulders back and braced her bare feet apart. "I don't want to waste my time and pizza if I need to find someone else who has the experience to teach me what I want to know. Are you up to the challenge or should I check with Whitey Ross. I'm sure he'd show me a thing or two."

Anger boiled up in Ed's craw. "You will do no such thing."

"In case you didn't hear me, I'm single, over twenty-one and capable of making all of my own decisions." She ticked off the list on her fingers. "I just thought that you might be a better choice, given you're not interested in me, and I can trust you not to take advantage. Any more than I deem necessary to learn, of course."

He carried the pizza into the small kitchen and laid it on the counter, immediately regretting his decision. Without the box to run interference, the tent his dick caused jutted out prominently. How could he talk Kendall out of this crazy scheme? He needed time to think through this, time to come up with some plausible reason she should abstain.

"You do realize having sex can lead to—"

"Spare me, will ya?" She rolled her eyes. "I had this conversation with my brother ages ago. I'm on the pill, I have my own supply of condoms, and you will not talk me out of this." She marched toward him, her breasts bouncing with each step.

Ed held his breath, his cock swelling even more the closer she came.

She stopped in front of him. "Are you in, or not?" She planted both hands on her hips and tipped her head to the side. Her determination made the light in her green eyes dance.

Ed wanted nothing more than to be in, all right. But she was Connor's *little sister*.

"Fine. I'll take my pizza elsewhere." She made a grab for the box, leaning past him, her arm sliding across his naked torso.

At the contact, Ed groaned and grabbed her wrist. "Okay, okay. I'll do it. Against my better judgment and barring any lightning bolts from heaven."

Kendall straightened, facing Ed, her breasts pressing against his skin through the thin tank top, the tips, poking out as though teasing him for being weak and agreeing to her scheme.

Was he out of his mind to agree to this? The little girl had definitely grown up. Hell, she sported what...a size D cup, more than a mouthful and... and...he sniffed. A light, citrusy scent curled around his senses, tempting him past redemption. Normally, he hated perfumes, found them usually too strong and annoying, preferring the natural aromas of living things like roses and horse manure. "What's that smell?"

"Must be my perfume. Do you like it?" She tipped her chin and pulled her long blond hair to the side, exposing the graceful line of her neck.

Oh, yeah, he liked.

Too much.

He grabbed her arms and set her away from him. "Quit wearing it. Wear something like Chanel or Candies. Your man should like that." *If he didn't gag first.* "And apply it thick."

Kendall frowned. "Are you sure. Don't you want to smell it again, just to be certain?" She closed the distance and stood on her toes, her body snug against him from her hips to her breasts.

Jaw tight, Ed fought the urge to press her even closer. His cock nudged against her belly as if taking on a life of its own. "Who is this guy?" Ed said through gritted teeth. He grasped her arms and pushed her a safe distance away from him and his randy dick.

She smiled down at the tent his towel made. "Are you always this...um...agitated after a shower?"

He glanced down at the embarrassing tent. "Yes."

"Why don't you lose the towel? I'll need to get used to seeing a man naked. You might as well be the man. One male body looks pretty much like the rest." Her lips twitched, her gaze rising from his stiff member up to his dropped jaw. "Don't you agree?"

"No." Ed's mouth snapped shut. "Not all men are built alike."

"So, how are you different from other men?"

He liked to think he was larger—hell, he'd seen other guys in the locker room after football practice—he had the right to think it. Looking down into little Kendall Mason's bright blue eyes, he coughed. "It's not just the equipment but what you do with it." He shook his head. "Really, are you seriously going through with this?"

Kendall pouted. "Absolutely. I think this is the real deal. I'm in love with a guy that doesn't quite know I exist. I need help attracting him and I don't want to risk screwing it up."

"If he doesn't love you based on your personality, the sex won't be enough. Why don't you try abstinence to begin with?"

"Ed, honey, for your information, I'm not a virgin anymore. I got my cherry popped way back when I was eighteen."

Ed's hands fisted, a surge of red-hot rage roaring through his brain, frying a few brain cells along the way. "Who popped your cherry?" He'd find the bastard and wring his virginity-stealing neck.

With a laugh, Kendall reached for a slice of pizza and sat on the edge of the kitchen table. Her legs parted, displaying the silky smooth skin of the inside of her thighs and the triangular wedge of her midnight black thong panties.

Ed's groin tightened even more, and he had to force himself to turn away before he did or said something that indicated the gutter where his mind had fallen. He couldn't get over the image of her pert little ass pressed against the smooth surface of his kitchen table. Ed spun toward the pizza box, grabbed a slice and stared at the shape—a triangle just like the wedge of fabric over Kendall's pussy. He bit in, his tongue slurping the sauce from the sides of his lips—warm, wet, tasty.

"Umm, this is orgasmic, don't you think?"

Kendall's voice was low, silky and spot-on with the way Ed felt at the moment. "It's pizza." He chewed and swallowed, dragging in a deep breath before turning back to face Kendall. "I can't talk you out of this?"

She shook her head, a splash of tomato sauce falling from her lips to the V between her breasts. She giggled, tugged her tank low and scooped the sauce out with a finger, and then looked up at Ed. "You like the sauce more than I do. Want it?" She held out her finger, dripping with the rich sauce that had been warmed by her breasts.

Ed's mouth opened automatically and he sucked her finger into it, licking off the sauce before he came to his senses and realized this was Connor's sister sitting on his table, practically naked, sticking her finger in his mouth and teasing him with triangular wedges. *Holy Hell.* He couldn't do this. Not to his friend, a man fighting for their country in Afghanistan.

Ed grabbed her hand and pulled the finger from his mouth, fully intending on telling her he couldn't, and wouldn't, give her lessons in sex. "Where do you want to start?"

Kendall grinned and clapped her hands. "Tell me what makes a man look at a woman twice."

Full breasts, miniscule tank tops and G-string panties. Ed shook his head. "A pretty smile. Guys like a woman who can make them laugh."

Her forehead puckered into a frown. "That's it? What kind of clothing? What about how she walks?" Kendall hopped off the table and walked across the floor. "Does a man like a woman with a little sway to her hips like this?" She walked sedately across the floor.

No matter how controlled Kendall walked, she was sexy, her hips swaying naturally from side to side. Dressed in nothing but a very loose tank top, that rode up her hips, exposing her ass, the strap of her G-string buried deep between her cheeks. Ed stifled another groan. "A guy would like that." Any man would be a fool or gay not to like what Ed saw.

"Really?" She turned, her brows crinkling again. "Or should I add a little oomph to the hips?" She vamped across the length of the tiny kitchen, one foot crossing over the other, her hips rocking from side to side in an exaggerated swing. Her bra-less breasts swayed, the nipples rubbing against the thin ribbed fabric.

Ed's mouth watered. His dick couldn't get much harder and not explode.

"You liked that, didn't you?" Kendall grinned. "I can tell." She touched the tip of the towel. "That's settled, I'll do that kind of walk to get his attention."

He pulled away from the tip of her finger. "No." Ed grabbed her hips to hold them steady.

"Why not?"

He tried to engage his brain, despite the rush of blood flowing to the lower regions of his body. "Too much of a good thing only makes you look easy."

"And being easy isn't a good thing?" She touched his naked chest with her finger. "Doesn't a guy want to know he stands a chance with the girl?"

His skin heated. Ed captured her finger, his body tense. "Yes, but not all at once."

"Okay then. Minimize the swing of my hips." She smiled up at him. "What about kissing? I've had some experience kissing. Seems most guys start with the tongue. Is that really the right way to begin?"

"Kissing?" Ed gulped. This was going way past anything he could imagine. Think of Connor. Breaking his promise and disappointing his best friend would make him less likely to lose control. "Okay." He closed his eyes and puckered his lips.

"Oh, Ed, please, you look like you're about to suck on a pickle. Be serious and show me what a real first-date kiss should be like." She planted her hands on her hips, pulling the tank taut over her breasts. "I'll bet Whitey would have no problem whatsoever showing me anything I want."

"Whitey has no finesse," Ed growled. "Okay, fine." He gripped her upper arms and pecked her lips with a very chaste, brotherly kiss. "That's good for a first date."

Kendall's brows rose and she crossed her arms beneath her breasts, lifting them up enough to emphasize the pointy tips. "Really, Ed? That's the best you can do for a first date kiss? I need to know what to expect? How to react?"

"A good knee to the groin would be perfect."

"I'm trying to get the man to fall in love with me, not hit me up with assault and battery charges."

Her full, lovely lips formed a straight line, which

on Kendall looked just as sexy as a smile. His determination to stay distant wavered.

"Either show me what to expect or I'll find a better teacher."

"Fine." Frustration exploded inside Ed and he cupped the back of Kendall's head crushing her lips with his. Kendall's mouth parted on a gasp, her tongue meeting his, twisting and stroking, the tang of tomato sauce whetting his appetite for more. She had him kissing her, something he would never have dreamed of, given his promise to her brother.

Her hands circled the back of Ed's neck, feathering through his hair. "How's this?" she said against his mouth. "Do you like this? Will my guy like this?"

"Umm." One hand slid down to cup her ass, pulling her hard against the terrycloth towel and his rock-hard erection. All that stood between his cock and her pussy was a towel, a string and a promise.

"Or, would he prefer this?" She nibbled at his lower lip, then slid her mouth across his chin and down to the pulse beating wildly at the base of his throat. Based on his heart rate and the erection, he couldn't deny his attraction.

So far, so good. But Lacey had said not to push him too far the first day. Go easy, make him want to come to her.

Oh, but she wanted more...now. For the past five years, she'd been in love with her brother's best friend, an awkward place to be. For most of that time, Ed had only seen her as Connor's kid sister.

This plan had better work and show Ed she wasn't a little girl anymore.

Reluctantly, Kendall pulled away from Ed and forced an innocent smile to her lips. "Would he like that?"

Ed scrubbed a hand down over his face, his eyes glazed, the point of his cock pressing hard against her belly. "Uh..." He shook his head. "No."

"No?" She feigned surprise. "What *does* get a man excited?"

"Getting naked." Ed's eyes rounded and he clapped a hand over his lips.

Kendall swallowed the big grin fighting for a chance to swamp her face. "Really?" She reached for the hem of her shirt and dragged it halfway up her torso.

Ed's hand shot out, stopping any further ascent. "There are other ways to get a man excited besides getting naked."

"I figured as much. Show me." She let go of the shirt and waited for him to make the next move.

"A woman's hands can be very sexy," Ed blurted.

"You mean like this?" She reached out and circled his cock, towel and all.

Ed sucked in his breath and disengaged her fingers. "Not quite that obvious, although that would get his attention all right. You might save that for the proposal night."

"What about this?" She ran her fingers up his naked torso, something she'd wanted to do for so long. The feel of his muscled skin was so good, she thought she'd died and gone to heaven. Her insides were on fire and she couldn't wait for this plan to take complete affect.

"Yes, maybe tweak the nipples."

She pinched his nipples ever so slightly. "You like that? I mean, a man likes that?"

"With the right woman, anything goes. I don't know why you need me to...to..."

Kendall leaned forward and nibbled his nipple with her teeth.

Ed stiffened, his breathing stopping altogether until she released the nipple. Then all of the air whooshed out of his lungs. "Baby, you don't need me to show you what a man likes."

"Oh, but I do. There's such a fine line between enticing a man and looking like a slut. This man is marriage material. I don't want him to think he can fuck me and ditch me." Her fingers skimmed along his shoulder and downward, weaving into the hairs on his chest. "I want *him* to want *me* enough to work for my affection."

"Okay then, save the nipple sucking for at least the fourth date."

She tipped her head. "Too much too soon?"

He nodded. "Yeah, too much too soon."

Kendall almost laughed. The man had a shell-shocked expression on his face, as if he didn't know how to react to Kendall's come-ons. She almost clapped her hands with her excitement, but she had a long way to go to make him want her badly enough to step completely over the line of loyalty to his best friend.

"Okay, then. Maybe tomorrow we can try the kissing again. I'm on my way to work at the Ugly Stick Saloon." She nodded toward the pizza box. "You can have the rest, but save me one piece I might be hungry when I get back. I have some studying to do late into the night."

"I'll be asleep," Ed said.

His words shot out a little too fast. Probably wanting to discourage her late-night visit. "Not to worry. I have a key. I'll let myself in." She twisted her shirt, making sure she pulled it tight enough to expose the full curve of her breasts. "Don't worry, I'll be very quiet."

His chest rose and fell, the muscle in his jaw twitching.

Oh, yeah, he was barely hanging on by a thread.

She nodded toward his towel. "You might want to do something about that. I'm sure it's not healthy to have a hard-on for that long." Kendall giggled and ran for the door.

The snap of a towel preceded a sharp sting to her butt.

"Ow." She jumped and spun in time to see Ed retracting the towel and holding it over his penis. "What was that for?"

"Forcing me into this crazy scheme of yours. You

haven't even told me who this guy is. I've a mind to have a talk with him."

"Oh, no. That wouldn't do at all. I don't want him to know I'm after him. He'd think I was a stalker or something."

"If you don't tell me who he is, I won't continue with the lessons."

"There's always Whitey."

He stepped forward. "I'll kill him if he offers."

"Then I'll find someone else and I won't tell you about him."

His mouth opened and snapped shut. "Brat."

"You love me and you know it." She blew him a kiss and fled through the open door, sure to give him a healthy look at her bare bottom.

If she wasn't mistaken, she'd made the man completely uncomfortable. Based on his continued hard-on throughout the session, the state was exactly the kind of uncomfortable she wanted him to be. Round one: Kendall 1, Ed 0.

CHAPTER THREE

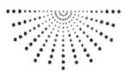

*E*d wadded the towel into a tight knot and flung it across the room. What was he thinking by agreeing to Kendall's crazy scheme? It could only lead to trouble, and he'd promised Connor he'd keep his little sister out of trouble until Connor made it back from deployment.

After a glance at his throbbing boner, he shook his head. Images of Kendall in the window, Kendall in her G-string panties and that damned see-through tank top kept flashing through his mind. He'd never get any relief at this point.

Maybe another cold shower would do it for him. Maybe two or three cold showers. Oh, hell, he didn't want a cold shower, he wanted a satisfying fuck. He grabbed his cell phone and spun through his contacts.

Allison? He shook his head. She'd gotten married two months ago to some guy from Austin.

Danielle? He hit her number and waited for the phone to ring. A piercing tone grated against his ear. "This number has been disconnected or is no longer is service."

Damn!

What about Frankie? Surely, she'd be home and wouldn't mind a quick tumble in bed. He hit her number and waited, his cock twitching.

"Yeah." Frankie answered on the third ring. Children screamed in the background.

"Hi Frankie, it's Ed."

"Oh, Ed, it's been a long time since I heard from you. What's up? Lindsey, put your brother down! Bryan, stop tormenting your sister!"

Ed held the phone away from his ear until the screaming stopped. He'd forgotten she had joint custody of her four children. "Your week to have the kids, is it?"

"Sure is, and Lance gave them to me all hyped up on sugar."

"You're busy. I'll call another time." He started to hit the off button.

"Wait, Ed, I'm free next Saturday. Wanna go out for old time's sake?"

Now that he had her on the phone, seeing Frankie didn't seem such a great idea. She had the grace of a biker babe and the shrill voice of a fishwife, especially when she was mad at someone. "Uh...I'm sorry, Frankie, I'm all tied up next Saturday. Maybe next time."

"Maybe so. Call me."

The hopeful, almost desperate, tone of her voice resonated with his own feelings. Wasn't he just as desperate to find a woman willing to jump in the sack at a moment's notice? Geez had it been that long since he'd gone out on a date? He flung his phone on the couch and marched to the bathroom. Giving the shower handle a vicious twist, he waited for the water to warm, then stepped beneath the spray.

Ed lathered up with soap then his hand closed around his aching dick, sliding up and down, thrusting long and hard, faster and faster until he burst over the edge, his body shuddering with the intensity of his release. Not the best release a man could have, but it would have to do. He had to do something about his lack of female companionship or these crazy, mixed-up sex education sessions with Kendall would kill him.

As he stepped out of the shower, he heard his phone ringing in the other room. God, he hoped it wasn't Frankie. Or worse, Kendall. After jerking off in the shower, he didn't want a repeat hard-on. He wrapped a towel around his waist and ran to catch the call, dripping across the floor. Ed pulled the phone out from under a throw pillow and checked the caller ID. Connor Mason flashed across the screen.

Damn.

Guilt gnawing a hole in his gut, he hit the talk button. Was it fate that had Connor calling tonight of all nights? Or was he psychic and reading Ed's lust-filled thoughts of his baby sister? Ed swallowed hard and forced a cheerful tone. "Hey, buddy, when you comin' home?"

Connor laughed. "I just got here a month ago, and the tour's for no less than fourteen months, you know that. Why? Things getting to you back home?"

"No, no. Nothin' like that. Just askin'." He ran a hand through his wet hair, trying to pull himself together. Connor needed to know everything was going great at home. He had enough to worry about dodging bullets in the Middle East.

"How's that kid sister of mine? Causing you any grief?"

Ed stifled the groan that immediately rose in his chest at the "grief" Kendall had caused him in the past two hours. Keeping in mind the need to keep Connor oblivious to any strife on the home-front, Ed gritted his teeth and lied, "No, not at all. She's being a perfect angel."

"Ha! Now I *know* you're lying."

Crap, he'd laid it on too thick. "Really, she hasn't dropped out of college, she's still working nights and I check on her every day. I'd know if something was up." Ed crossed his fingers and prayed his friend wouldn't question him about Kendall's love life.

"What about guys? Is she seeing anyone?"

"She may have a crush on some guy from one of her classes."

"Really?" Connor's voice tightened.

Ed could kick himself for even mentioning it. "Yeah, they study together at her place."

"Damn. She needs to finish her degree before she gets involved with some jerk."

"Not to worry." Not to worry much, and not at all if Ed could help it. "I'm keeping a close eye on her."

"Got a feeling it'll take more than that. Kendall is too pretty for her own good. She doesn't need to be alone with a guy. You know guys are only thinking about one thing—gettin' some."

Ed's cock throbbed in agreement. "Yeah, pretty much. Although I really think they're studying." But he wasn't sure and he couldn't be sure unless he was at the house all the time. "Besides, she's twenty-one and legal. She can do whatever she wants. No matter what we say."

"I know. I just wish I was there to advise her." Connor sighed. "That's why I asked you to look out for her. She respects you and turns to you like a brother. I know I can trust you to take care of her."

That wad of guilt twisted in Ed's gut. "You can count on me, buddy."

"Do me a favor, will ya?" Connor asked.

"Yeah, anything?"

"Check out this guy. Let him know her brother carries a big gun and has friends who'll take him out back if he doesn't treat Kendall nice."

"Will do."

"Well, I gotta go. Tell Kendall I said hello. I'll try to call when she's not at work. Damn, I miss you guys."

"Same here." Ed missed his friend. Right now, the best he could do for Connor was assure him that he'd take care of his only living relative, Kendall. He ran a hand through his hair. "Don't worry about Kendall, I'll make sure she stays out of trouble."

"Thanks, Ed. I feel better already."

Ed could hear voices in the background over the phone line.

"Hey, Ed, I gotta go. We're moving out for patrol."

His mouth dried and he swallowed hard. "Stay low and come back safe." Ed's words sounded so trite, but he meant them from the bottom of his heart.

"I plan on it. I don't know when I'll get the chance to call again. I will as soon as I can. Later."

Ed hit the off button and stared down at the cell phone, more depressed than when they'd started their conversation. Connor was like the brother he never had. He and Kendall were the only family he had since both his parents had died. If anything happened to Connor...Well, that possibility didn't bear thinking about.

Not one to wallow in depression, Ed pulled on a clean pair of shorts, a t-shirt and jogging shoes. He'd worked hard all day at the ranch and didn't need the exercise to keep in shape. Instead, he needed to walk, to get out and think through everything that had happened that day.

He set off down the street, casting a quick glance up at Kendall's apartment window above his. She'd be at work now, serving beer and shooters to patrons of the Ugly Stick Saloon. Would her new boyfriend be there, waiting to see her after work? Ed walked faster, the frustration he'd felt earlier returning instead of receding.

Kendall was headstrong, stubborn and beautiful. A killer combination to try to keep up with. The kicker was that she had every right to do whatever the hell she pleased. Ed could do nothing to stop her. If he told her not to do something, she'd probably go out and do it, just to spite him. His only option for coming between her and this mystery boy was to plant himself right in the middle. If they didn't have time alone together, they couldn't build a relationship. And they sure as hell wouldn't have time to get it on.

If playing the part of Kendall's sex education teacher kept her too busy to pursue her new love interest, so be it. He'd take on that responsibility, no matter how many cold showers required to get through it or how many times he had to masturbate.

By the time he turned and headed back to the house, he realized he'd been walking for over two hours. He might actually sleep better, but he'd be exhausted at work the next day. At least, his libido had calmed and he wasn't thinking of a naked Kendall anymore. Just the comfort of his bed where he planned to fall to sleep immediately.

As Ed approached the house, he noted the light on in Kendall's window. The shade was drawn, but he could see her moving around, the silhouette of her body clearly outlined. She reached behind her back and unclasped her bra, letting it slide down her arms.

Ed groaned. He didn't need to see that. All the walking he'd done to get his lust back in line just flew out the window. His cock sprang to attention, pressing against the thin fabric of his jogging shorts. *Holy Hell.* The next thirteen months would be the death of him.

With heavy resignation, he trudged up the steps and entered the house, going directly to his apartment and an icy cold shower.

KENDALL STRIPPED NAKED and stepped into the shower. Tuesday nights tended to be slow at work and her boss had sent her home early. She'd had far too much time to think through her first sex education lesson with Ed, and she didn't know if she could maintain a teasing distance for long. Lacey assured her that keeping Ed on the edge was a surefire way to make him want her as much as she wanted him. With the added jealousy angle with a potential boyfriend in the background, she'd have his love, or at the very least, Ed's lust in the bag, or sack, by the end of the week.

In the meantime, her body ached with a need so powerful, she thought she might explode if she didn't get some relief.

The warm shower spray only made her hotter

and more excited as soap suds sluiced over her breasts and down her ribs. Her fingers brushed over her nipples, the taut, nubs begging to be suckled by a man. One man...Ed.

Her hand slipped lower, the soap slick and smooth, catching in the fluff of hairs over her pussy. How she'd love to have Ed's hands stroking her as she stroked herself. She parted her folds, flicking at her clit, pretending it was Ed's tongue, lapping at her core, drinking in her juices, nipping and nibbling at that oh-so-sensitive bit of flesh, over and over, until she screamed out her release.

Kendall could imagine taking a sudsy shower with Ed. Naked, foaming, incredibly hot. He'd push her up against the cool tiles, wrap her legs around his muscular waist and thrust into her, hard and fast, his cock thick, stretching her channel, their bodies sliding together under the shower's spray. They'd make love until the water turned cold, then he'd dry every inch of her body, and carry her to his bed where they'd make love all night long.

Oh, sweet Jesus. She couldn't wait until her next lesson.

Kendall turned off the shower, grabbed for a towel, barely even dried her body as she headed for the door to her apartment. When she yanked open the door, she yelped and jumped back.

Lacey stood with her hand raised ready to knock. Her brows rose and her gaze swept the length of Kendall's naked body. "Going somewhere?"

"I have to have him now. I can't wait." Kendall pushed past Lacey but was stopped by an elbow hooked into her arm.

Lacey yanked her to a stop. "Oh, no you don't."

Her skin cooled as the air dried the water droplets. "But I can't remain celibate for an entire week, when he's right downstairs." She tugged against the arm holding her. "Let me go."

"No way." Lacey put herself between Kendall and the staircase and pushed Kendall back into her apartment. "Take a deep breath and tell me what happened with Plan B."

Kendall stared at her apartment door, her blood raging through her veins. The fact that she stood in front of her friend without a stitch of clothing on should have been an indication she was losing it. She was past caring, her rampant desire pushing her to the brink of sanity. "I'm on fire." Kendall's hands crossed over her breasts and ran down to the apex of her thighs. "All I can think about is him taking me, again and again. This sex education plan is making me even more crazy than before. How is that helping me?"

Lacey took Kendall into her arms and hugged her. "Shh, baby. It'll be okay."

"How, when all I can think about is sex? I barely functioned at work, I can't focus on homework. I couldn't even shower without getting the female equivalent of a hard-on. I need him." Kendall wailed. "Now!"

"What you need is a good vibrator with fresh batteries."

"No, I need Ed, his cock between my legs, fucking me like there was no tomorrow."

Lacey's eyes widened. "My, my. We are in a tizzy, aren't we?"

"I'm going down there." Kendall headed for the door again. "Don't get in my way."

"Okay, go ahead." Lacey crossed her arms over her chest, her lips pressing into a thin line. "And if you go down there like you are now, you'll frighten the poor boy into the next county."

Kendall's hand closed around the doorknob before she froze. "Sweet Jesus." She leaned her head against the wood paneling. "I can't take this."

Lacey's hand smoothed along her back. "Let me help you take the edge off."

Kendall turned and leaned against the door. "How?"

"Close your eyes."

Kendall looked at her friend skeptically then shrugged. "Fine, whatever." She closed her eyes and waited. "But I don't see how that's going to help."

"Just pretend I'm Ed." Lacey's lips closed around one of Kendall's taut nipples, sucking the tip into her warm, moist mouth.

Desire tugged at Kendall's core, and her eyes opened wide. "What are you doing?"

"Saving you from making a big mistake." Lacey grinned up at her. "You liked that, didn't you?"

Kendall frowned at Lacey, but she couldn't deny it. "That doesn't make me love Ed any less."

"I don't want you to love him less, and I have no intention of stealing you away. I'm just helping you keep your sanity until phase two of Plan B." Lacey tweaked the hard little button on the tip of her nipple. "Now shut up and close your eyes again. I'll even lower my voice if that helps."

"No, no." Kendall sucked in a quick breath as Lacey's lips closed on the other nipple and she bit down gently. Her breasts flushed, and swirling heat gripped her low in the belly. "This is doing it."

"Good." Lacey continued to suckle on her breasts.

Kendall moaned. "This is only making me hotter."

Lacey straightened, her brow furrowing. "I guess there's nothing to it but to give you the works."

Kendall's heart skipped several beats. "The works?" she said, her voice breathless, her pussy creaming at the thought.

Lacey pulled her shirt up over her head and dropped it where she stood. She turned her back to Kendall. "Would you get the clasp on my bra?"

Was Lacey a lesbian? She'd always shown interest in sexy men. This was Kendall's first inclination that her best friend might have different tastes in sexual partners.

The thought titillated Kendall. She'd never been with a woman before. She reached out and unhooked the bra while Lacey shimmied out of her denim skirt, revealing a decadent lack of panties, her smooth, creamy ass bared to Kendall's view.

"Oh, this can't be right," Kendall whispered.

"Why not?" Lacey faced her, a hand on her hip, her full, rounded breasts pushed out, ripe and ready for tasting. "You need release, and it's been a long time for me too. What's wrong with helping out each other? We're friends, aren't we?"

"I've never been with a woman."

"That makes two of us." Lacey's lips twitched. "But when you marched through that door all wet and naked..." She shrugged. "I have to admit, you turned me on." She held up her hands. "Don't worry, it's just a sex thing. I know how much you love Ed, and I'd never do a thing to come between you two. But damn, girl, I'm so horny I could die."

"Well...your breasts are...wow...gorgeous...and I am...fuckin' hot, but..."

"Wait." Lacey held up her hand. "Hold that thought. I have something that will help."

She tore open the door and raced across the hall and into her own apartment. The cool night air filtered through the open door, curling around Kendall's breasts and pussy, making her excruciatingly aware of her own nakedness. And damned if she didn't like it. Maybe she'd walk around naked more often.

Lacey returned in seconds, carrying a bright silver thick dildo, no less than a foot long. "Watch this." She twisted the bottom and the dildo vibrated. "It has five speeds."

"You actually own one of those?"

With a raised brow, Lacey looked at Kendall. "Doesn't every girl? Good grief, Kendall. I've got to take you shopping." She grabbed Kendall's hand and led her to the bedroom. "Get in the bed."

Kendall dragged her feet. "I don't think I can do this."

"Well if you can't, will you at least watch so I can get myself off?" Lacey held the vibrating dildo between her breasts, the motion making her boobs jiggle. "Please."

CHAPTER FOUR

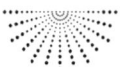

endall couldn't tear her gaze from the jiggle of Lacey's breasts. When she should have been saying, *hell no*, her mouth opened and she said, "Okay, just this once, and only because I'm still so keyed up I won't sleep anyway."

"Oh, baby. That man has you tied in knots. Let's start by getting you relaxed. Lay down on your stomach and I'll rub your back." Lacey turned Kendall toward the bed and gave her a nudge.

Not entirely comfortable with getting in bed with a naked woman, Kendall lay down on her stomach, her body tense, not fully convinced this was a good idea.

Lacey switched off the dildo and laid it on the bed. "We can do that later." She straddled Kendall's hips, the fuzz of her pussy brushing against Kendall's buttocks, sending shockwaves throughout her body.

Tension and heat filled Kendall's core, drenching

her pussy with desire. *Sweet Jesus*. She was lusting after a woman—her friend, no less. She shot a glance over her shoulder at Lacey. "I have a feeling that after tonight, I won't be able to look at you the same."

"As long as you respect me in the morning." Lacey laughed and squirted lotion onto her hands. "If you don't make a big deal out of it, you'll be fine." She rubbed her hands across Kendall's shoulder. "How's that?"

Kendall moaned. "Magic. I need this every day after work." Her friend's hands slipped lower, rubbing lotion into the middle of her back.

Lacey scooted down over her legs and bent closer, her breasts sliding over Kendall's shoulders. "I'm game if you return the favor."

"I'm halfway to considering it." Kendall surprised herself by her response.

"Can't leave you halfway there." Lacey slipped lower still, her fingers skimming across Kendall's lower back to the rounded curve of her ass.

Kendall's tension went to an entirely different level. Part of her wanted Lacey to keep it impersonal, the other part wanted her to take it a step further.

Lacey's fingers slid down the line of Kendall's ass.

That move wasn't impersonal. Kendall sucked in a breath, too shocked and turned-on to say anything. She lay there, letting her friend do what she was doing, helpless to stop her. Unwilling to try.

With the tip of her finger, Lacey traced the tight ring of her ass. Then her finger slid to Kendall's pussy where she swirled it around and around the opening until she had it nice and wet.

Her breath catching in her throat, Kendall couldn't resist hiking up her ass.

"That's right, honey, come up on your hands and knees. It'll be so much easier." Lacey rose to stand on her knees between Kendall's legs.

So far gone to the far side of girl-on-girl sex, Kendall rose to her hands and knees and waited impatiently for whatever Lacey had in store next.

"Mmm, you're pussy is so pretty."

Kendall laughed. "And you would know this *how?*"

Lacey snorted. "I have videos and a mirror. I know what a pussy looks like."

"You have videos?" Why was it she didn't know these things about her very best friend?

"Oh, sweetheart, you have so much to learn. Make a note to have our own Sex Ed show you his collection."

Kendall looked back, her brows rising. "How do you know he has a collection?"

"Seriously?" Lacey shook her head. "Trust me, he has a collection." She slid her finger in and out of Kendall's vagina. When her finger was slick with juices, she traced a line to Kendall's asshole. "Ever been finger-fucked in the ass?"

Kendall's ass puckered, her core tingling in antici-pation. "No." Kendall said, sure she was about to experience it.

"Be sure to have Ed do this when you two finally

get together. It'll feel even better with bigger..." she pressed her finger into the hole, "...fingers."

All the air in Kendall's lungs whooshed out. "Wow." A rush of juices drenched her pussy.

"Pretty cool, huh? Wait, it gets better."

The hum of a miniature motor filled the air and Kendall looked over her shoulder. "What are you doing?"

"What do you think I'm doing?" Lacey pressed the vibrating dildo to Kendall's clit, while her thumb slid into Kendall's pussy.

With the vibrator stimulating her clit and Lacey's thumb in her pussy and her finger in her ass, Kendall couldn't talk. Every breath she took hitched and released before it could make it into her lungs. "Sweet Jesus. That feels so good."

Lacey increased the pace, thrusting her finger and thumb in and out.

Tension spread from her core throughout her body as Kendall moaned and cried out, "Yes! There! Oh, God, yes!" Right on the edge of orgasm, Lacey's sweet torture ended abruptly.

"Oh, please." Kendall's body sagged, her pussy still tingling. "Don't stop now."

Lacey slapped Kendall's ass. "I have no intention of stopping now. But I want some of this too." She lay down on the bed, head pointed to the foot of the bed, opposite of Kendall. Lacey scooted close, lifted Kendall's knee and slid her head beneath Kendall's pussy. "Now, we both get to have a little fun. And remember, the louder the better. Count it as all part of the plan to make Ed wish he was the one." Lacey nudged Kendall's knees wider and wider until her pussy hovered over Lacey's mouth.

A warm breath of air blew across Kendall's hot wetness. A groan rose from her throat as she stared down at Lacey's furry mound.

"Go ahead, touch me. But I'll warn you, I'm ready to come any moment." Lacey let her knees fall to the side, the light brown hair curling over her folds, springy and tempting Kendall.

Balancing on one hand, she parted the folds to find Lacey's clit, the little sliver of flesh making her curious. Kendall knew what turned herself on. She flicked the nubbin with the tip of her finger.

Lacey's heels dug into the mattress and her ass lifted off the bed. "Oh, baby, do that again," she moaned.

The folds were warm but dry. Lacey's clit needed more lubricant to make it easy to rub. Kendall leaned forward, hesitant but driven by her own need for release. She touched Lacey's clit with the tip of her tongue. She tasted mildly of scented body wash and womanly musk. Kendall licked the length of her clit and sucked it into her mouth.

Lacey pressed her feet into the mattress again, thrusting upward, forcing Kendall to take more. At the same time, she parted Kendall's folds and tongued her clit, flicking and licking her until

Kendall squirmed, her knees scooting wider, pressing her pussy closer to the source of sweet torture.

"Oh my god, that feels so good," Kendall moaned, breathing a stream of air over Lacey's pussy, much as Lacey had done to hers. She licked Lacey's clit, while pressing her finger into her thoroughly drenched pussy. The pace of her tongue matched that of Lacey's, increasing the tempo and force of her thrusts.

Lacey's fingers clutched at Kendall's ass, her tongue sliding into Kendall's pussy and then returning to her swollen, throbbing, sensitive clit.

Kendall's body tightened like a bowstring, every nerve on fire, her focus centered on the crazy things Lacey was doing. She found that the whole effect intensified when she followed Lacey's lead, repeating her moves until Lacey cried out, "Yes! There! Oh, God, yes!" Her friend's body tensed, pelvis thrusting spasmodically, fingernails digging into Kendall's skin.

Kendall teetered on the edge, that final climax within reach, her body ready.

Lacey reached for the dildo, switched it on and thrust it into Kendall's pussy. Her tongue stroked her clit while the vibrator filled her channel, the overwhelming sensations catapulted her over the edge, her mind and body exploding with wave after wave of her orgasm. Her breathing grew ragged and her arms and legs shook.

When she finally came back to earth, Kendall

collapsed on the bed beside Lacey, the dildo still inside her vibrating. "I gotta get one of these."

ED LAY on top of his bed, wearing nothing. He usually slept in the nude, but tonight he couldn't even lie beneath the sheets. The slightest bit of friction against his dick had him rock hard in seconds. That's what that little brat upstairs had reduced him to—a quivering mass of hypersensitive nerves. He couldn't masturbate every time he got a hard on, he'd wear out his hand and his cock. The inside of a vagina was so much softer and lubricated just right.

Ed groaned and glanced over at the clock. Midnight and he was still awake. How in hell was he going to work tomorrow without sleep?

A dull thud made his head jerk up off the pillow. It sounded like it came from Kendall's apartment above him. Then another thump reverberated through the ceiling, followed by a low moan.

Ed leaped out of bed and strained to hear more. Was someone in Kendall's apartment? He was halfway to his bedroom door when he heard another moan, and the soft sound of feminine laughter. What the hell was going on up there?

If Kendall was laughing, she wasn't being attacked. But the moans...

Another moan preceded a muffled scream, "Yes! There! Oh, God, yes!"

Kendall was making love with someone in her apartment.

A flash of rage ripped through Ed, surprising the hell out of him. He marched across his living room, ready to rip a new asshole out of the guy who'd crossed the line.

Ed hadn't gone a day from his most recent promise to get in the way of Kendall and her new lover and he'd already failed. More than that, Ed couldn't stand the thought of Kendall lying beneath another man, his cock inside her, fucking her. Making love to her when Ed himself couldn't.

No fucking way!

His hand closed around the doorknob before he came to his senses enough to realize he couldn't go up there and confront the man while he himself was still naked. With a jerk, he grabbed his jogging shorts from where he'd left them on the living room floor and jammed his legs into them as he pushed through the door. Taking the steps two at a time, he made it to the top in record time and slammed his fist against Kendall's door. "Kendall Mason, open this damned door."

A long pause ensued.

Ed hammered on the door again. "Kendall, come open this door."

The door opened and Kendall stood with a sheet loosely wrapped around her, toga-style.

Her appearance hit him in the chest. Her blond

hair was mussed and sexy, her cheeks pink with a faint blush.

"Ed?" She glanced over her shoulder and closed the door a little. "What are you doing up here?"

"Get him out."

"Get who out?" Kendall's brows furrowed. "What are you talking about?"

"The man in your bedroom. Get him out." Ed pushed against the door, fully intending to march into Kendall's bedroom and throw out the bastard.

Kendall planted herself in front of him, her hold on the door firm. "First of all, I don't have a man in my bedroom. Second...I'm twenty-one and can have a man in my bedroom if I choose to." The edge of the sheet slipped down, revealing a dusky nipple. She hiked the corner of the sheet back up to cover herself.

But the damage was done.

Ed's cock sprang to life, his entire body on fire with anger and lust. "I'll count to five and that man better leave before I kick his ass from here to tomorrow. One..."

"Ed, I'm warning you."

"Two..."

"You aren't my father."

"Three..." His hands fisted.

"This is ridiculous."

"Four..."

"Ed Judson...is that you making all that noise out here?" Kendall's friend, Lacey appeared in the doorway, dressed in jeans and a T-shirt, her hair pulled back in a ponytail, her feet bare. "Wanna join the party? We were just watching a video." Her lips twisted into a sexy, secretive smile.

All of the air left Ed's sails and he stared at Lacey, his brow wrinkling, wondering what the hell was going on. "Is there a man in Kendall's bedroom?"

"No men in here?" Lacey stepped to the side. "You can come look if you want. Oh, Kendall, quit teasing the man. Let him in."

Kendall's eyes narrowed. "As long as he understands, that he doesn't have the right to chase men out of my apartment."

Lacey waved Kendall's words aside with a flick of her wrist. "Ed understands, don't you, sweetie?"

He didn't respond, his brain working hard to determine if he was being had or not.

"Whatever, come see for yourself." Kendall shifted the sheet and held the door wide.

Ed strode across the room and peered into the bedroom. As far as he could see, there wasn't a man anywhere in sight.

"Want to check under the bed and in the closet?" Lacey asked, standing in the doorway.

Ed turned sideways and squeezed between Lacey and the doorframe, rubbing against her breasts in the process.

A devilish smile curled her lips.

When he made it through, a sharp sting bit into his ass. He spun, gaze narrowed.

Lacey's hand fell to her side. "Sorry. I just had to know if it was as hard as it looked."

"And?"

"Oh, it is, all right." She winked at Kendall and laughed.

Ed squatted beside the bed and looked beneath. Nothing there but Kendall's shoes and a plastic storage container.

"Don't forget the closet. A girl can hide a lot of sin in a closet," Kendall prodded, standing beside Lacey, still holding that damned sheet over her nakedness.

Uncomfortable with the two women watching him, Ed opened the closet door to a mass of shirts, pants, dresses and shoes. There were boxes and belts, a bicycle helmet, basketball, volleyball and just about everything else under the sun...except a man.

"Satisfied?"

The sarcasm in Kendall's voice couldn't be mistaken. Ed turned and faced the women across the bed, defeated. Confusion spun through Ed's mind. He didn't have a clue what was going on. "If there isn't a man in that bedroom, what was all that moaning?"

That's when he saw it. Light from the bedside table glinted off its sleek silver casing, winking at him like a beacon in a sea of rumpled sheets. He'd almost rather have found a man in Kendall's bed than that.

A man he could pick up by his scrawny neck and kick his ass out with a great deal of pleasure.

A vibrator would remain unchallenged,

untouched by Ed's hands and left behind in a room with two women. *Holy Hell.*

Kendall's lips turned up in a Mona-Lisa-smile. "Were we keeping you awake?" She pressed a hand to her mouth, her eyes widening. "I'm sooo sorry. We were just getting into the movie. We promise to keep it down from now on."

Ed glared at Kendall, wanting to say something, but his brain couldn't put words to his thoughts. Finally, he managed, "Do that. I have to work in the morning."

"We'll be quiet." Kendall moved away from the door, motioning for Ed to follow. "I wouldn't want you to be too tired for tomorrow night's lesson."

Sex education was the last thing Ed wanted to think about before he attempted to sleep in what was left of the night.

Kendall walked him to the door and held it open, a smile playing around her lips. "I hope to use tonight's lesson on my guy tomorrow. I'll be sure to let you know how it goes." She started to close the door, clearly indicating an end to his visit.

When Ed didn't move, she looked at him wide-eyed. "Is there something else?"

Ed stared down into the eyes of a woman he wasn't sure he knew anymore. She sure as hell wasn't the kid sister of his friend. No sirree, she'd grown into a woman, full of mischief and feminine wiles. "No. Just keep it down." He turned and left.

If he wasn't mistaken, Kendall giggled as she shut the door.

What the hell was that about?

And what was Lacey doing in Kendall's bedroom while Kendall was wearing nothing more than a sheet? And whose vibrator was that on the bed? What were they doing with it while watching a movie?

If he thought images of a naked Kendall were enough to keep him up all night, the images inspired by the two women together doomed him to sleeplessness for the week. *Holy Hell.* Why did Connor have to get deployed now? Why couldn't he wait until his little sister was safely married off to some farmer?

Ed stomped down the stairs to his apartment and slammed the door behind him.

For the next hour, he paced his bedroom floor, his ears straining to hear what was going on upstairs. Other than a few loud giggles, the thumping had stopped. At one point, he thought he heard the faint hum of a tiny motor. But that could have been his overactive imagination.

What was Kendall up to with Lacey? And why was she interested in a man when she was doing God-knows-what with a woman?

His mind still spinning, Ed stripped out of his shorts and laid on top of his sheets, his dick hard as a rock, the clock displaying bright green as if mocking him. *One-fucking-thirty in the fucking morning.* Ed couldn't believe he was lusting after Kendall Mason

—his best friend's little sister. He had half a mind to pay a visit to the doctor for a mild sedative to keep him from getting a boner every time he was near Kendall. Was there such a thing as anti-Viagra?

And to think, some men couldn't get it up. Not Ed. He couldn't keep the poor boy down. He lifted his head. Moonlight shone off his stiff cock. Giving it a silver sheen much like the dildo in Kendall's bed.

Holy Hell.

CHAPTER FIVE

*F*or the tenth time, Ed paced the length of the barn. He'd yet to round-up his horse, much less saddle him for the day's work. His eyes burned from lack of sleep and he'd taken not one but three cold showers during the night to shake the effect of Kendall's crazy request. Not to mention the silver vibrator mystery he wasn't sure he wanted to know about.

"Hey Ed, I thought you'd be out in the pen with Ranger by now."

"I should be." He performed a sharp about-face and marched to the other end of the barn, away from Grant.

"My, my. I don't think I've ever seen the great Ed Judson this riled. What's eating you?" Grant leaned against a stall door and crossed his arms over his chest.

"Kendall Mason."

"Is she out carousing with an undesirable?"

Guilt and desire warred in Ed's gut. "I can't say."

"Spit it out."

"No, it's something I gotta work out for myself."

"Suit yourself. I'm here if you need to talk." Grant grabbed a bridle and was almost out the door when Ed broke.

"She wants me to give her sex education lessons," Ed blurted out through clenched teeth.

Grant spun to face Ed, his brows practically meeting his hairline. "She what?"

"You heard me. She wants me to teach her how to attract a man, what a man likes from first date to all-the-way."

Grant stood with his jaw hanging down around his chest.

"Damn it, Grant, shut your mouth before I put a fist in it!" Ed spun on his boot heels, grabbed a bridle and headed out to the corral where Ranger awaited his scheduled morning exercise.

"Wait, wait," Grant trotted to keep up with Ed. "Let me understand this. You mean to tell me little Kendall Mason asked *you* to teach her all about what a man likes?" Grant removed his hat and ran a hand through his hair. "So what's your problem? You've been handed a gift from God."

"The Devil's temptation is more like it." Ed kicked at the ground. He needed a fight, wanting to punch something or someone. "I'm not fit to train horses in my current state of mind."

"Tell me how you managed to land this gig, I want one of my own."

"Not with Kendall, you don't." He glared at his boss and flung the bridle over the fence rail. "I didn't ask for it. She propositioned me and threatened to take her request to Whitey Ross if I turned her down." Ed slapped a palm on the rail so hard it stung.

Ranger flung his head back and trotted to the far side of the pen.

"Hell, I'm not fit to train horses today."

Grant laughed. "No, my friend, you'll get yourself thrown at this rate." The older man leaned his arms on the top rail of the fence and grinned out at Ranger. "Kendall Mason asked you to give her lessons in sex."

Ed growled.

"You know, she's not a baby anymore."

"You think I didn't notice?" Ed tipped his head backward, his eyes closed to the morning sun. His mind replayed Kendall's breast peeking out from the poorly wrapped sheet, the line of her G-string panties disappearing between her butt cheeks, the way her nipples poked at the thin fabric of her tank top. "Hell, she's a full-grown woman."

"With the figure and desires to prove it." Grant shook his head. "Think she'd go out with me?"

He sucked in a breath through his nose before speaking. "I'm a hair's breadth away from landing my fist in your face, boss or no boss."

Grant held out his hands in front of his face and

laughed aloud. "Sorry, just had to poke at you. You're wound tighter than a bowstring."

"You have no idea. I don't think I slept more than fifteen minutes last night."

"Maybe you should take the day off."

"No. I need to do something to keep my mind off Kendall and the lessons she'll expect from me tonight." Ed leaned his forehead against the fence rail, pressing against the rough wood. "I promised Connor I'd look out for her."

"Wow, you are in a bind."

"Yeah. I'm damned if I give her what she wants, and damned if Whitey takes over."

"Did she say why she wanted lessons?"

Ed's frown deepened, a snarl curling his lip. "She's hot over some guy and wants to use the lessons to attract his attention."

"Did she say who the guy was?"

"No. But I think I have an idea." He swallowed hard against a tight throat. God, he hated to admit this. "She's been studying with some jerk from her college. I see him leaving as I get home from work."

"Maybe you need to get home early and check it out." Grant slapped a hand on Ed's back. "Personally, I'd love to be in your shoes, buddy. Kendall is one hot little filly."

"Grannttt," Ed warned.

Grant raised his hands again. "I'm just saying. She's a grown woman and fair game in the eyes of every male in town. I'm surprised she's held off this long from latching onto a man. Can't be from lack of some guys trying. You're a lucky dog that she picked you."

"Yeah, but Connor trusts me to look out for her, not fuck her. And she only wants sex education lessons to help her land another guy." A burst of red-hot rage slammed through his bloodstream, surging its way straight to his chest. "I gotta find out who this guy is and tell him to fuck off."

"Be careful, Ed. Sometimes telling a guy to back off only makes him want the girl more. It could back-fire on you."

"I don't care. Connor's only been gone a month. A goddamn month! I have thirteen more to go before I can walk away from this stupid promise."

Grant looked out across the paddock. "Don't know what to tell you. A cowboy's word is his honor."

"Yeah." Ed drew in a long breath and let it out slowly. "That's the problem. That and some randy boy poking around Kendall while she's as hot as a cat in heat."

"Stop. You're getting me all worked up." A grin spread across Grant's face. "I can just picture Kendall in that tight little jean skirt she wore the other night serving at the Ugly Stick Saloon." Grant shook his head. "She had every male in the building panting after her."

Ed groaned. "You see what I have to put up with?"

"Yeah, I don't envy your promise. Plus, I really

don't see a way around these lessons you're supposed to teach her. How will you show her what a man likes without actually...showing her?"

"I was hoping you had some suggestions." Ed looked at his boss hopefully.

"Short of buying a blow-up doll with anatomically correct parts, I can't think of a thing."

"A blow-up doll?" Ed's brows rose. "Can I get one of those from that adult shop out on the county line?"

"I'm almost positive they'll have them. I know they have the female dolls. Not so certain about the males." Grant shook his head. "Really, though, you should just go for her body."

"What?" Ed stared at his friend. Had he lost his mind? "I can't do that, she's Connor's *little* sister."

"Are you attracted to her?" Grant's gaze locked on Ed's,

His boss's stare refused to let him shy away from the answer to that loaded question. "Damn it, yes." Ed looked out across the barnyard. "That's the problem. She's too damned pretty for my own good."

"Does the attraction go deeper than just the physical?"

His chest tightened, breathing becoming more difficult, and his head swam. "What do you mean?"

"Do you love the girl?"

"Of course I do. She's Connor's sister."

"No, do you L.O.V.E. the girl? As in willing to take her to the altar kind of love?" Grant stared hard.

A stare lasting long enough to make him squirm. Ed looked away first. "I don't know."

"Think about it. Can you see her dating another man without getting mad about it?"

"No."

"Can you picture her in bed with someone other than you?"

"Hell, no." Ed shoved his hand through his hair, his body tense, visions of Kendall lying naked in bed rampaging through his head. *Holy Hell*, he wanted her. And he didn't want any man planting himself inside her. "Hell, no," he repeated.

Grant shrugged. "Then go for her. Connor will understand and probably be happy she'd settle for his best friend, rather than a low-life like Whitey."

"I don't know if I'm ready to commit." Ed shook his head. "And I'd bet my leather chaps Connor didn't have *fuck my sister* in mind when he said take care of Kendall."

"Yeah, but if you told him about Kendall's little deal and Whitey, he'd switch gears really quick."

"I don't know. I talked to him last night. He was going out on maneuvers, probably getting shot at. How can I tell him anything that will have him so worried his head wouldn't be in the fight?" Ed leaned back against the corral fence.

"You're right. He doesn't need the worry." Grant's lips twisted. "Do you think your attraction to Kendall is more than because she's pretty?"

"I don't know. I spent most of my life thinking of her as a sister."

"And now?"

Ed's shoulders sagged. "Not at all. She's not the same kid in ponytails and she's got great..." He held his hands out at breast level, his thoughts on the perfect shape and size of her boobs. Then he remembered where he was and who he was talking to. "...skin. She's got great skin."

Grant laughed. "Go for the girl. You have it bad for her already."

Ed hooked his thumbs in his back pockets and stared at his boots. "She's having me show her what a guy likes for some other dude, not me."

"Then in the process of showing her, let her see what a great catch you are."

Ed snorted.

"As far as I see it, you got two choices. Check out the doll situation at the adult toy store, or go for the girl. Either way something's gotta give."

"Yeah."

"In the meantime, how about pounding some T-posts? There's a fence down on the northern edge of the ranch. Do some manual labor to burn off some of that testosterone."

"You're right." Ed smiled at his boss and friend. "Thanks. At least, I have some options to think about."

"Yeah, and I'll have a very vivid image of Kendall Mason in her tight skirt, asking you to give her sex lessons to keep me warm all day in this ninety-degree weather." Grant's lips pressed into a line. "Not sure I'm going to make it to lunch."

"She was wearing a tank top and thong panties." Ed's eyes narrowed. "But get your mind out of the gutter with my girl."

"Your girl, is it?" Grant's eyes widened. "Getting territorial all the sudden?"

"Shuddup." Ed nodded at Ranger. "You got him?"

"Yeah, take the four-wheeler for the day." His boss laughed. "I don't think any of the horses would put up with you today."

Ed gathered a pole pounder, T-posts wire and ties, loaded them onto the four-wheeler and headed out across the ranch, the wind blowing in his face, the sun warming his skin. Yeah, pounding a few T-posts would help for a while. At least until he got home that afternoon, after a detour to the X-rated Adult store on the county line.

NEAR THE END of the day, Ed was hot, sweaty and exhausted, certain he'd have no trouble fighting his desire for Kendall. Especially with a blow-up doll he hoped to pick up on the way home.

His first stone wall hit him square in the face when the lady at the adult store told him they only carried the female blow-up dolls. If he wanted, they could order a male, but it would take two weeks to get it in.

Kendall wouldn't wait two weeks for him to continue lessons, she'd pull up stakes and march on over to Whitey's to continue her education.

His frustration made him angry. By the time he reached the house, he was in no mood to see Kendall's window wide open, music blaring loud enough even Old Man Frantzen could hear it, and that blond-haired gigolo gyrating to the beat in nothing but a pair of fancy leather chaps and a G-string.

Ed's blood pressure shot through the roof. He slammed his truck into Park and leaped out before the engine had a chance to come to a full stop.

Kendall swung into full view through her window, twisting and gyrating to the music like one of the buxom dancers at the Ugly Stick Saloon on a Friday night.

Ed took the stairs two at a time, tripping on the last one when his boot missed it and slipped down a step. He racked his shin on the corner of the top stair and issued a string of curse words that would have made his mother wash his mouth out with soap for a week.

"Ed?" Lacey flung open her door and stepped out. "Are you okay?"

"I'm fine, just clumsy. He picked himself up and dusted his hands on his dirty jeans. "What the hell's going on in Kendall's apartment?"

Lacey smiled. "She's having a little study session with Cory."

"Study session, my ass." He raised a hand to pound it against the door.

Lacey grabbed his wrist before he could. "Hey, before you go breaking up her fun, I wanted to talk to you."

The music inside the apartment was so loud the walls shook. Ed couldn't think past his desire to strangle the dude inside dirty-dancing with Kendall, much less have a conversation with Lacey over God knew what. "What." The one word shot out like a bullet, sharp, and to the point.

"You like Kendall, don't you?" Lacey inserted herself between him and the door, garnering his full attention.

"Yeah, she's my best friend's sister. I've known her all my life."

"You've known her, but have you *known* her since she's now all grown up?"

Ed's groin tightened. "What's your point?"

"You're not her brother, and that's bothering you, isn't it?"

"I'm her brother's best friend. He asked me to keep her out of trouble." Unease skittered along his skin. What was she leading up to?

"Does he know you're in love with her?"

Ed staggered backward and almost fell down the steps. "What are you talking about?"

Lacey grinned and her eyes danced. "You don't even realize it yourself, do you?"

"I can't love her, she's my—"

"—best friend's little sister." Lacey waved his words aside with a flick of her hand. "Does she look like a little girl?" The woman shook her head and poked a finger into his chest. "No. And she's not. She knows what she wants and isn't afraid to go after it. She learned that from you." Tilting her head, Lacey planted a fist on her hip. "So what are you going to do about it?"

"About what?" Ed's head spun. How could he make astute trades in the stock market amassing a small fortune in a short amount of time, but he couldn't begin to understand the workings of a woman's mind?

A loud sigh echoed in the hallway. "Kendall. What are you going to do about Kendall?"

"She's in love with some jerk. Probably the guy in her apartment right now." Ed pushed forward, his determination renewed to break up Kendall's little dance party.

Lacey laid a hand on his chest. "Breaking them up isn't the way to win Kendall."

"No, but I'd get great satisfaction from punching the boy's lights out."

"And Kendall would love him all the more for taking the fall." Lacey shook her head. "Did you ever think Kendall might still think of you as her other big brother?"

"Yeah. So?"

"If you want her to see you as a potential lover,

you have to show her how incredible it the chemistry could be between the two of you."

"You mean make love to her?" Ed shook his head, his heart hammering double-time. "I promised to keep her out of trouble, not get her into it."

"No, no. You need to make her notice you by being with another woman. That way she would see you as a very desirable man, not at all a brotherly figure."

Ed's brows pulled together. "Wouldn't that just make her jealous?"

Lacey shrugged. "Yes, possibly. Just depends on how you present it."

Ed scrubbed a hand through his hair, standing it on end. "I'm just a dumb cowboy. Spell it out before I grow old, will ya?"

With a laugh, Lacey leaned back against Kendall's door. "I know Kendall asked you to give her sex education lessons."

Ed couldn't meet Lacey's direct gaze, not liking where this conversation was going. "Yeah, and?"

"And you're probably feeling uncomfortable having her practice the things a man likes on you."

"More like...frustrating...go on." Intrigued, he forced the music out of the forefront of his mind and listened to Lacey. Maybe the woman had a solution to his problem.

"What you need is a demo dummy."

"I thought of that." Ed crossed both arms over his chest. "I tried to find a blow-up doll at the adult store. They were out of male models. It'll be two weeks before they get one in."

"You're on the right track, but I have a proposal even better than that." Her lips curled into a secret smile.

Ed braced himself.

"What you need is a live model."

"That's me." Ed poked a thumb at his chest.

"Right, but you need a live female model to demonstrate with so that Kendall won't be demonstrating on you." A grin spread across her face and she held out her hands, like a magician having pulled a bunny out of his hat. "What do you think?"

"That you're crazy as hell, and I'm even crazier for listening." Ed nodded toward the door. "Move, or be moved."

"Promise me you'll think about it. At the least, you don't break your promise to Connor. At best, you make Kendall jealous enough to notice you as the hunky cowboy you are."

Ed breathed in and out several times before he finally spoke. "Fine."

"You'll do it?" Lacey's face lit with a big smile.

"No. I'll think about it."

Lacey nodded. "Fair enough."

The door behind Lacey jerked open and she fell backward into the blond guy's arms. "Oops!" She smiled up at him. "Hi, Cory."

"Hey, Lacey." Cory helped her to stand on her

own then stuck out his hand. "You must be Ed. Kendall's told me all about you."

Ed glared at the young man with the light blond hair and shirtless body. With all the restraint of a pit bull on a leash, he held out his hand. "Sorry to say she hasn't mentioned a word about you." His fingers tightened around Cory's in a punishing grip.

Kendall stepped up behind Cory, her brows raised. "Ed? You're home early."

"Apparently not early enough. I was just saying hello to your friend."

Cory's face turned a deep shade of red, his body bending under the pressure on Ed's grip. "Yeah, just saying hello."

With a frown, Kendall said, "Ed, let go of Cory's hand."

"Of course." He immediately released his grip, a smirk tugging at his lips as the boy shook blood back into his fingers.

"Look, I gotta go." Cory smiled at Kendall. "We're on for tonight, right?"

"It's a date."

"Great. See you then." Cory eased past Ed, hurried down the stairs, and the front door slammed shut behind him.

Kendall crossed her arms over her chest, her eyes narrowing. "What are you two doing out here lurking in the hallway?"

Lacey leaned into Ed. "I was just asking Ed if he'd

give me sex education lessons along with you. You know, a two-fer deal?"

Ed opened his mouth to tell Lacey what she could do with her deal then stopped. The frown pressing Kendall's pretty brows together had him rethinking Lacey's offer.

"Two-fer?" Kendall stared from Ed to Lacey and back.

"Yeah." Lacey draped a hand on Ed's arm. "Two-fer-one. I volunteered to be his dummy so he could show us both what a man really wants."

Kendall's frown deepened.

A thrill of excitement sped through Ed's veins and he made his decision. Having Lacey as his personal dummy might just work on either front. If Kendall was interested, she'd be jealous. If she wasn't, Ed would be guilt-free with his buddy, Connor.

And it would give him time to sort through his own feelings for Kendall.

CHAPTER SIX

"*How* long until you're ready for our lesson?" Kendall directed her question to Ed. Anger warred with anticipation; anticipation winning. She'd deal with Lacey after Ed left.

"I need a shower. Give me thirty minutes. Are you providing dinner?" He grinned.

The man looked far too happy about the situation. "I'll figure out something. Go on and get your shower."

Ed winked at Lacey. "See you in thirty minutes."

"Can't wait." Lacey smiled brightly.

Kendall gritted her teeth, wanting to scratch out her ex-friend's eyes.

Instead, she pasted a smile on her face and wiggled her fingers at Ed, her gaze following him to the bottom of the stairs. She held her tongue until his door shut with a thud behind him. Then she grabbed

Lacey's arm in a punishing clutch and yanked her into her apartment, slamming the door. "What the hell are you trying to do? I thought you were my friend?"

"I am, sweetie." Lacey winced at the fingers squeezing her arm. "Mind letting up on me so I can explain?"

Kendall's hands dropped to her sides, her fists clenching and unclenching, her chest rising and falling with each angry breath. "Start explaining, and this better be good."

Lacey smiled. "It is. It'll work out perfectly."

"Yeah, yeah, you haven't gotten to the part where I agree." Kendall crossed both arms over her chest and stood ramrod straight. "Continue."

"Ed was hesitant to touch you, wasn't he?"

Hadn't they already discussed this? Kendall's skin tingled with impatience. "So, the plan was for him to give me sex education lessons, and get used to the idea."

"But don't you see?" Lacey waved a hand. He's torn by his loyalty to your brother. Involving me in the Sex Ed lessons gets him used to the idea of being with you."

Kendall shook her head. "I'm not seeing it."

"Just give it a chance. If it doesn't work out the way you think it should, I'll back out. No harm, no foul."

Kendall stared at her friend for a long time before she sighed. "One lesson. Then I call it."

"Fair enough." Lacey hugged Kendall. "You'll see, this'll all work out."

Kendall remained stiff. "I don't know. I feel more like I'm losing ground with Ed than gaining."

"Look, let's make a bet."

"I don't need a wager." Her shoulders slumped. "I need Ed."

Lacey smiled. "I bet you ten dollars that by the end of this week, that one-hundred-percent-red-blooded-hubba-hubba male will be all yours."

Kendall hoped so. She'd loved him so long. When she'd set out to win over Ed, she'd promised herself that if the attempt didn't work out, she'd move on. She'd have her degree in a month. If she and Ed weren't together, Kendall had plans to move to Austin and get a life without the man.

"What have you got in your frig that would feed a man with a big appetite?" Kendall asked.

Lacey clapped her hands. "You won't regret it, Kendall."

"I hope not. I'd hate to lose a friend."

Her friend headed for the door. "I have a casserole I can pop in the microwave and have it ready in fifteen minutes." She stopped and faced Kendall. "Did you make up the banana pudding like I told you to?"

"Check." Kendall had it chilling in her refrigerator.

"Spray can of whipped cream?" Lacey asked.

"Check."

"Cherries?"

"Check." Kendall shook her head. "I don't know why we need dessert. Ed rarely eats dessert."

"Oh, honey, he'll be all into it tonight." She smiled and flounced out the door. "Oh, and wear that sleeveless cotton blouse that's so sheer you can see through it with your micro-mini denim skirt. No under things." The door closed behind her, the last three words echoing through Kendall's living room.

No under things.

Her pussy creamed in anticipation of the next sex lesson with Ed. If all went well, she'd see a little action tonight.

Kendall raced around the apartment, digging through her closet, searching for the skirt and sheer blouse. When she couldn't find them immediately, she had a near panic attack. Then she remembered hanging them on the back of the bathroom door, just for this occasion. She stripped naked, tucked her hair up in towel and stepped beneath the shower's spray, rinsing off the sweat from her dance session with Cory.

He was coming along much quicker than she'd anticipated. So quickly, she knew he'd be ready for Ladies Night tonight.

After her lesson with Ed, she planned to make it to the Ugly Stick for Cory's debut performance. The women were going to love him. Kendall had taught him all of the best dance moves she'd observed from the men who came every week for Ladies Night.

Lacey had assured her that going to Cory's debut

wouldn't set her back on her campaign to win over Ed. She'd insisted this early in the plan was too soon to stay the night with Ed.

Kendall wasn't so certain. She wanted to spend every night with Ed. For the rest of her life, starting now.

Turning the shower setting to cold, she rinsed off the body wash, the chill making her nipples pucker nicely. She shoved aside the shower curtain and squealed when she noticed the clock. She had only two minutes to comb her hair and dress. She wanted to beat Lacey to Ed's apartment.

Still slightly damp, she yanked the denim skirt over her hips and shimmied into the floral, sleeveless cotton blouse, only buttoning the middle three buttons. Barefoot, she raced through the door and teetered at the top of the stairs when Lacey's door opened and she emerged carrying a casserole dish and wearing a form-fitting ribbed knit tank mini dress that wasn't much more than a shirt barely covering her ass.

A burst of rage roared through Kendall. "Remember, he's mine."

Lacey laughed out loud. "Oh, honey, I know that, and I wouldn't dream of taking him from you. Not that I could. You look absolutely yummy in that outfit. I can see your nipples plain as day. It's perfect." Her brows furrowed. "Where's the dessert?"

"Damn, I forgot." Kendall spun, racing for her apartment, fully aware Lacey would now arrive at

Ed's before she could gather the pudding, whipped cream and cherries. Why did she have to be so forgetful?

Her feet slowed. What was she worried about? Ed and Lacey wouldn't start without her...would they?

Kendall grabbed the dessert items and ran for the stairs, almost tripping over the first one. She righted herself and took a deep breath. This was insane. Lacey was her friend. She wouldn't come between them.

Forcing herself to calm, she descended the steps carefully and knocked on Ed's door. As soon as her knuckles hit the wood, her pulse raced and her breathing grew more ragged. Session two of Sex Ed was about to begin.

A full minute elapsed from the time she knocked before Kendall gave up and twisted the knob.

Lacey's laugh could be heard from Ed's kitchen.

Anger pushed Kendall forward. When she rounded the corner, the sight before her made her want to throw the pudding, whipped cream and jar of cherries right at Ed and Lacey.

Lacey leaned up on tip-toe, reaching for plates in the cabinet, her dress hem rising high enough to expose one naked butt cheek. Ed stood behind her, damned near on top of her, reaching high to gather the plates. The fan over the stove roared over a tray of burned toast.

Neither of them had heard her enter.

Ed reached the plates before Lacey and pulled them from the cabinet.

Before he could back away, Lacey spun to face him, laughter shining from her face. "I could have gotten them."

"Face it, you're short." He laid the plates on the counter, then swatted Lacey's fanny. "But nice ass."

Lacey laughed and grabbed for the plates. "Thanks." When she turned toward Kendall, she grinned. "Hey, K. About time you got here. We're hungry and ready to eat."

That wasn't all they were, but Kendall held her tongue, reminding herself Ed thought she wanted to learn about sex to entice another man. She wasn't supposed to be after him. The idea was to make him jealous enough to want her.

Her brows knit. And whose idea had that been?

Lacey's.

And whose idea was it to be a sex dummy for the Sex Ed lessons?

Lacey's.

And who was the patsy here?

Blood pounded in her eyes. Kendall suspected she was being played.

Well, she didn't plan on letting Lacey have her way with Ed. Friend or no friend, Kendall had plans of her own for the night. And top on her list was to show Ed just how sexy and grown up she'd become, even if it meant jumping over Lacey to get to him.

Lacey loaded a plate with the casserole and

handed one to Kendall. She loaded another and handed it to Ed. "You two go on into the living room and get started. I want to make another stab at toast. Hopefully, not burning it this time."

Ed grabbed forks from the drawer and nodded at Kendall. "Come on. I'm starving and this smells good enough to eat. That Lacey is a great cook."

A knot formed in Kendall's gut. Strike one up for Lacey. Kendall couldn't cook her way out of a pizza box. She stared after Ed as he left the kitchen.

"What are you waiting for? Don't you know food can be very sexy?" Lacey gave her a push.

"Casserole?" Kendall stared at the chicken with gooey cheese sauce on her plate.

"Honey, any kind of food. Go on, get started without me."

"I don't get it."

"Good lord, girl. Use your imagination. Drop some somewhere suggestive."

Kendall carried her plate into the living room and sat on the couch with Ed, her mind spinning around Lacey's suggestion. She lifted a forkful of casserole, a string of cheese stretching from her plate up to her fork. "What are we going to cover tonight in our lesson?" How was she going to make this look sexy? She popped the food in her mouth and chewed.

Ed's hand paused on its way to his mouth. "How about how to make a man hot while on a dinner date?"

For once, they seemed to be on the same page. Kendall smiled. "Enlighten me."

"Start by licking the cheese off your lips."

His voice rasped in her ears and heat rose in her cheeks. "How embarrassing."

"Not at all. Not with the right man. One who can envision the possibilities."

Kendall slid her tongue out along her lips.

"Slowly." Ed's blue eyes flared, his own tongue sweeping out across his own lips as slow as he wanted her to. "You missed it. Here. Let me." He leaned close and pressed both lips to her lower lip, sucking it in.

At his touch, Kendall's heart skipped several beats then crashed against her ribs.

He nibbled at her lip and released it, a smile spreading across his face. "Your turn. Try something different."

Kendall dipped her fork into her food, dizzy from the last demonstration, but determined to pass this lesson with flying colors. She aimed to drop a little of the cheese sauce on her chest, but it wouldn't slip easily off her fork. With a little jerk, she tried flicking it. A glob of chicken and cheese jumped in the air and landed on her thigh, at the edge of her skirt hem and then the warm mixture slid down between her legs.

Her eyes widened, her breath hitching in her lungs.

"I'd say you're catching on quickly." Ed cleared his

throat. "Allow me." Eyelids lowered, he bent toward her.

Kendall 's legs parted automatically, the anticipation of Ed licking the cheese sauce off her inner thigh more than she could have dreamed of so soon into the lesson.

"Look at you two, getting off to a roaring start without me." Lacey carried her plate into the room.

Ed straightened, a slow red burn rising up from the collar of his black T-shirt.

Once again, Kendall could kill Lacey for even being in the same room.

"If you're not going to get that, let me." Lacey laid her plate on the coffee table and slid a finger over Kendall's thigh, scooping the cheese from her leg. She held it out to Ed.

Without a moment's hesitation, the man sucked the finger into his mouth and licked it clean.

Kendall sat silent, stunned, turned on and furious all at once. If Lacey hadn't entered the room, Ed just might have licked that cheese off the inside of her thigh.

"Let Lacey show you the one where you drop something down your cleavage. A man goes wild for a woman's breasts." Ed turned to Lacey and nodded. "Do it."

Lacey took a forkful of cheese sauce and tipped it carefully.

Of course, the cheese slipped right off her fork

and landed as pretty as you please in the cleavage between her breasts.

"Oops." She batted her eyes at Ed.

Kendall gripped her fork, ready to stick it into Lacey's leg.

"Perfect." Ed grinned. "If you and your guy are alone, you can ask him to help you out like this." He leaned close to Lacey.

Lacey tugged on the neckline, drawing it down low enough to display the trail of cheese sauce.

Kendall leaned forward to see what he was doing, half-jealous, and fully excited.

Ed braced his hands on Lacey's rounded breasts and licked the cheese from between them, coming up smacking his lips. "See? Easy and the act gets a guy off like nothing you can begin to imagine."

"Let me try." Kendall dug her fork into her plate.

Scooting back on the couch, Ed shrugged. "No need. I think you have the hang of it."

"No, I want to get it right, and practice makes perfect," Kendall insisted. She swirled her fork around her plate, searching for the perfect combination of wet and cheesy sauce.

When she lifted the fork, the cheese dripped off before she could make it to the V of her shirt. Instead, the glob landed on her nipple. "Great." She looked up at Ed and grimaced. "I can't even spill food right."

Ed's gaze zeroed in on the drop of cheese. He didn't respond to Kendall's lament. The muscles in his neck worked several times before he cleared his throat and looked up. "No, baby, you got it right." He leaned over and sucked the cheese into his mouth, nipple and all through the thin fabric of her shirt.

Kendall's back arched, pressing the breast closer to Ed, her breath hitching in her chest. Oh, yeah, she'd gotten it right. Her hands reached out for Ed's head to hold him closer.

Before Kendall could dig her fingers into his hair, Lacey giggled. "Kendall gets an A for effort on that lesson. Ready for dessert?"

Ed's mouth released Kendall's nipple and he straightened. "Well, done," he said, his voice rough. "And yes, let's move on. I believe you brought dessert?"

The loss of his mouth's warmth sent a pang straight through her core. Kendall could easily have shot Lacey right between the eyes. She'd been so close to...to...to what? Having Ed suck on her boob? Okay, so he'd gone past kissing, that was a step in the right direction. But when would he take her to his bed and make love to her into the night? She wanted to move the lessons along a lot faster than Lacey had dictated. But she didn't want to appear to be easy. She was supposed to be learning all this to entice another man. Well, in Ed's eyes. The added jealousy angle.

"Your guy will definitely like the food on the boob trick."

Ed patted her back like a big brother patting his

little sister. So much for jealousy. Kendall wanted to strip off her clothing and stand in front of Ed and say, "Look at me! I'm a woman and I want you." She actually reached for the buttons on her blouse when she glanced across at her friend.

Lacey shook her head. "Go get the dessert, we won't need bowls or spoons."

"For pudding?" Kendall tipped her head sideways.

"Trust me. We won't need them."

Ed grinned across at Lacey, sending another bolt of green-eyed envy through Kendall. Why couldn't he be that sexy and natural around her? What was she doing wrong?

She trudged to the kitchen, returning with the pudding, spray can of whipped cream and the jar of maraschino cherries.

Lacey sat so close to Ed, she was practically in his lap.

Kendall set down the dessert items with a thump on the table.

"Thanks, Kendall." Ed stuck his finger into the banana pudding, dipped out a nice, big dollop and stuck it in his mouth. "Umm. That's perfect for what I had planned next. We're stepping up the pace on the lessons. We'll assume you are past the first few awkward, getting-to-know-you dates. I think you can get through the kissing and dinner. Remember to progress slowly. Men don't like a woman to come on to them too strong at first."

"Really?" Kendall caught herself before snapping,

you could have fooled me. She waited until Ed wasn't looking then glared at Lacey.

Lacey had the gall to wink at her.

"As I was saying," Ed continued. "We'll move right into the first bedroom contact."

Kendall plopped down on the couch next to Ed. "Now, you're talking."

"You're ready for the next lesson?" Ed nodded toward the dessert. "A man likes it when a woman tastes sweet, no matter where he tastes her. Lacey, if you would, dip a finger into the pudding and stick it into your mouth."

"I've been dying for some of this." She dipped her finger into the pudding and poked it into her mouth.

"Hold it there and make it look like you're having an orgasm."

Lacey's eyelids drooped and she thrust her finger in and out of her mouth, moaning softly.

"Good. Very good." Ed watched her a moment longer then turned to Kendall. "Now, Kendall, dip your finger."

She did.

"Now put it in my mouth." Ed smiled. "Go ahead."

Kendall pressed the tip of her pudding-drenched finger into his mouth. At the same time, her own opened, her tongue sliding across her suddenly dry lips.

He sucked her finger into his mouth, tonguing the pudding with firm licks. When he had it cleaned, he pulled back. "Dip again."

His blue eyes glowed with an intensity Kendall couldn't resist. She dipped her finger into the pudding and raised it to his lips.

He kept his mouth closed and shook his head, his body so tight already he couldn't imagine taking this lesson any farther. But he would.

"No." He guided her finger to the side of her neck and spread pudding down to the base of her throat where her pulse beat erratically. His gut clenched, his penis throbbing painfully. She was aroused as much as he was.

"If a man is interested, he'll see this as an offering and accept, like this." He cupped the back of her neck, tugging at her hair, pulling her head back to expose her throat and the long line of pudding. He licked the pudding from just below her chin, down the column of her neck to the base where he lingered, tonguing the pulse beneath her pale skin.

"I do believe you two have that one down."

Kendall's eyes narrowed.

Ed straightened. "Right. Lacey, your turn. Dip out some of the pudding."

She did and held out her finger.

Next to him, Kendall frowned, leaning into him, her gaze on Lacey's finger.

Ed guided Lacey's finger to her thigh and ran it from the inside of her knee to the hem of her dress. "Now it gets more interesting. When a woman traces a path of sweets along the inside of her thigh, the act tells a guy she's ready for the next step. Come and get me."

With his large, calloused hands, Ed parted Lacey's legs. He dropped to his knees and moved between them, dipping his head to lick the pudding from her knee along her inner thigh, nudging the hem of her dress upward with his nose. "Ah, perfect." He lifted the dress and looked over his shoulder at Kendall. "No panties."

CHAPTER SEVEN

Kendall squirmed next to Ed, her own denim micro-mini skirt edging upward. She'd had enough of this cat-and-mouse teasing with the pudding. "Let me try that." She dipped her finger into the pudding and touched some to her lips first. She leaned close and kissed Ed. "Like this?"

Ed's tongue swept out to lick the pudding off Kendall's lips. "Ummm. Yes."

Now if this doesn't get you hot, I don't know what will. With the rest of the pudding, Kendall spread a line from the middle of her inner thigh up to the hem of her skirt, pushing the denim higher to expose the mound of hair over her pussy. Her finger, with the remaining pudding, slipped between her wet folds. "Like this?"

Again, Ed's tongue swept across his lips. "Ummm. Yes."

"Oh, let me." Lacey pushed past Ed and she dropped between Kendall's legs, her pretty pink tongue lapping up the banana pudding all the way to Kendall's pussy. "Oh, yes, I can see how this would get a man off. It's got me *all* excited. "

Too shocked to react at first, Kendall watched as her friend licked the pudding off her skin, Lacey's mouth moving toward her clit. Her pussy creamed, her body trembling.

A hand clamped down on Lacey's shoulder. "I'll take it from here." Ed pulled Lacey away from Kendall, his eyes more stormy gray than blue, his mouth set in grim lines, the shorts he'd worn for the occasion tenting out magnificently.

Kendall hid a satisfied smile.

As Lacey moved back, she winked again at Kendall.

For the first time that evening, Kendall could actually forgive Lacey for coming between her and Ed.

"A man would be crazy not to respond to an opening like that." He lifted one of her heels from the floor and placed it on the couch, spreading her legs wide. Then he lay down between them, his tongue going directly to the pudding, lapping at her clit until every sweet drop was gone.

Pulses rippled along her folds. Kendall's back arched, her fingers lacing through his hair, drawing him closer. "Oh, yes, that's what I want."

"Here, let's try some whipped cream while we're

at it." Lacey slipped her hands between Ed and Kendall and flipped the three buttons free on Kendall's shirt, peeling the edges open. Holding the can of spray whipped cream over a breast, she squirted a circle around the nipple, building it up to a point.

The cool cream tightened her nipple even more.

Ed moved up Kendall's body.

"Wait, we're not done yet." Lacey reached behind her and plucked a cherry from the jar, placing it on the tip of the nipple whipped cream. "Now, enjoy your dessert."

Kendall barely heard the door open or close as Lacey left the apartment. Her attention remained riveted on Ed. He crawled up her body like a man on a mission, his eyes glazed, his body hot, his cock pressing between her legs, still constrained by the gym shorts.

He plucked the cherry from the tip of the whipped cream, then proceeded to lick every last drop of the white fluffy sweetness from her breast. "This is the best part." He took her nipple between his teeth and rolled it.

Sharp pangs of longing shot throughout Kendall's body. The sensations were great, but they weren't enough. She wanted all of him, inside her, thrusting hard and fast. Kendall reveled in his attention to her breasts, but she wanted more.

Her hands came up between them and she shoved

him to arm's length. "I get the idea. But does it work both ways?"

Ed stared down at her, pausing as his eyes focused. "What?"

"Does it work both ways?"

His gaze locked on her breasts, and he shook his head. "I'm sorry. I don't know what you're talking about."

"Get off of me and let me show you."

He leaned back, allowing her to slip from beneath him. Once she made it off the couch, he collapsed onto his back, draping an arm over his face. "I'm sorry, Kendall, I shouldn't have let it go that far. I don't know what would have happened if you hadn't stopped me."

Stopped him! Kendall could have kicked herself into tomorrow. If she'd messed up her chances, she'd never forgive herself. "I have no intention of stopping you."

Ed peeked out from beneath his arm. "No?"

"No." She reached for the elastic band of his shorts and tugged them downward.

His hand captured hers before she got far. "What are you doing?"

"I told you." She tugged his hand loose and continued to pull the shorts over his hips. "I want to see if it works both ways." Before he could protest further, she yanked the shorts lower. "I've never been with a man and whipped cream at the same time. The idea intrigues me."

Ed's cock sprang free, jutting straight up. Oh yeah, she had him excited. Now if she could keep him that way until she fulfilled her own fantasy. She dipped a finger in the pudding and slathered the sweet along the length of his dick, rubbing the pudding up and down with both hands.

"Oh, baby." Ed moaned. "Do you know what you're doing?"

"Having dessert and eating it too." She grabbed the whipped cream can and sprayed a cone on the tip of his penis. Finally, she topped her creation with a bright red cherry. "Does a man like this as much as a woman?"

"It's kind of cold."

"Hmmm. Then let me clean it off." A smile played at Kendall's lips as she leaned over him, starting with the cherry. She plucked it into her mouth, chewed it quickly and swallowed, "Ummm, very nice. Anything yet?"

"Still cold, shrinking a bit."

Kendall snorted. He wasn't shrinking. He was much longer and thicker than the boys she'd played at making love with while growing up. She cupped his balls, aiming his cock for her lips then sliding it into her mouth, and an explosion of flavors burst across her tongue. Banana pudding and whipped cream…and Ed. Her tongue swirled around the hardened length, flicking against the mushroom tip.

"That's better. Much better."

Oh yeah, definitely. She released his cock, licking

the whipped cream from her lips. "Would you say it's as enticing as a woman spreading sweets between her legs?"

"Oh, yes." He laced his fingers into her hair and drew her down to him, thrusting his dick into her mouth.

Kendall smiled inwardly as she sucked his cock, slipping up and down over him, enjoying the smooth slide.

Until his body tensed and he pulled free of her mouth.

"I'm not wearing panties," Kendall reminded him. She held up a foil package she'd slipped into the back pocket of her jean skirt. "I'm ready to move on to the next lesson."

Ed snatched the condom from her and tore it open with his teeth. He sat up on the couch and started to apply the contraceptive.

Kendall took the rubber from him. "I need to know how to do this properly." She slid the dome over his reddish head and down his length, her fingers slipping along, warming it as she went. God, he was huge, hard and thick.

Her pussy creamed in anticipation. She straddled his legs, placed a knee on either side of his hips, coming down over him, her channel so slick with juices he slid right in.

Ed closed his eyes as he eased into her, his face tense, his hands on her ass guiding her.

Dear, sweet Jesus, this was exactly where Kendall

had hoped to go with this lesson. Heart beating wildly, she moved up and down over him. "Is this right? Or does the guy prefer to be on top?"

"Most guys don't care if they're on top, on the bottom or standing up as long as they're getting some." His eyes opened and his hands held her still, fully sheathing him. "Who is this guy you're after? Will you be doing this with him?"

Now was the time to own up to Ed that he was the one. The intensity of his stare had her balking. Tightening her thighs, Kendall rose up and slid down over him again. "Does it matter?" There, answering a question with a question would delay her having to own up to loving him. She needed to know how he felt about her before she admitted her love. In no way did she want him feeling sorry for her.

"Any other positions I should use that are particularly exciting to a man?" Kendall leaned close, flashing her breasts in his face, arching her back. Then with a great deal of restraint, she dismounted and stood in front of him. "I've never tried it, but I hear doggy-style can be quite enticing." With her skirt still hiked up over her hips, her pussy wet and warm from him, she dropped to her hands and knees on the couch beside Ed, presenting her bottom toward him.

Ed smoothed a large, rough hand over her cheeks. "I'm going to hell for this. I know it."

"No, you're not. You're helping a friend. Now is it better for the woman to be up on her hands like this or should she lean low, like this?" She dropped to her elbows, her ass jutting up, praying Ed would take her up on her blatant offer and not run screaming.

"You are so very beautiful." Ed moaned and pressed a kiss to her bottom. That one kiss was followed by another. "Connor is never going to forgive me."

Why had he mentioned her brother? She glanced over her shoulder at Ed. "What does Connor have to do with this?"

He avoided eye-contact. "Uh, he's my best friend and I'm about to...ah hell...you're his sister. I'm supposed to protect you, not fuck you."

Was that what had been holding him back? A need to protect Connor's baby sister? Kendall should have had a long talk with her brother before he'd left for the war. He needed to understand she wasn't a kid anymore, and Ed was the man she'd loved for so long she compared all men to his standard. "Ed Judson, what Connor doesn't know, won't hurt him. Besides, if it wasn't you helping me in my research..."

"It sure as hell wouldn't be Whitey." Ed scooted closer. He dipped his finger in the pudding and spread it along the crease between her butt cheeks, then licked his way along the seam, his tongue tracing the tight ring of her ass. "I'll never look at banana pudding the same."

The gentle glide of his tongue on her ass was more than she could have imagined, the sensations burning a path straight to her pussy. As her body clenched, Kendall sighed, a smile tilting the corners of her lips.

Ed might be reluctant because of his friendship to Connor, but he couldn't resist what was right there ready to be taken.

His tongue moved lower, delving into her pussy, trusting in and out. Then he was on his knees, his cock pushing into her, his hands gripping her hips.

"Yes. Oh, sweet Jesus. Yes!" Kendall called out, her fingers curling into the couch cushion as Ed rode her hard and fast, slamming into her with enough force to make skin-on-skin smacking sounds.

There was nothing gentle or tender about the way he fucked her. It was primal, hot, monkey sex and Kendall loved it, her own body tensing along with his, rising to the most incredible climax imaginable, teetering on the very edge of the ultimate release.

Ed thrust into her once more and stopped short of delivering. He held her hips for a long moment, buried inside her, then yanked out his cock, flipped her on her back and plunged into her with one final breath-stealing trust. His body froze, his dick pulsing inside her, his head flung back, eyes squeezed shut. Then he collapsed on top of her, crushing her with his weight.

Kendall didn't care that she couldn't breathe, she could die right now. She'd already gone straight to heaven in Ed's arms. Her hands rubbed along his muscled back, realizing he still wore his T-shirt. She wished he'd been naked so that her breasts would press firmly into his chest. She could easily lie here all night in Ed's arms. Hadn't she dreamed of this for years?

Ed pushed up to his elbows and stared down at Kendall. "Just who was teaching who on that lesson?"

"Why, you were teaching me, of course." Kendall smiled up at Ed and pushed a strand of hair off his forehead. It fell back as she let go. "Do I get an A for our lesson today?"

"You get an A+. You're a natural." Ed pressed a kiss to her lips.

"Thanks." Kendall pulled his head down to her and ran her tongue along the seam of his lips, tasting banana and sex. Then she pressed in, past his teeth to stroke his tongue. "You taste wonderful."

"So do you." He traced his finger along her jaw line and down her neck to the swell of her breasts. "When did you grow up?"

Kendall loved every callus on Ed's fingers. He'd earned them working hard on the Rocking G Ranch, doing a man's work. "I've been grown up, you just couldn't see anything but the little girl in ponytails I used to be."

"You're not a little girl anymore." He bent to take one nipple into his mouth, sucking on it gently, rolling the tip with his tongue.

"No, I'm not." Shivers of pleasure tickled along her skin. Kendall took a deep breath. This was the time to tell him that she was in love with him, that she wanted to be with him always. "Ed—"

A loud banging on the door made Ed's head come up.

"Who the hell is that?" Ed frowned at the door, making no move to get off of Kendall to answer it.

That had to be a good sign.

Another loud banging was followed by Lacey's voice. "Kendall, did you forget?"

Eyes narrowed, Ed stared down at Kendall. "Forget what?"

"Kendall, did you forget you had a date with Cory?" Lacey called out, her voice only slightly muffled by the solid wood door.

Kendall groaned. "I did forget." Her brows furrowed as she stared up at Ed. "I have to go."

In a fluid movement, Ed stood, reaching for his shorts. "You have a date?"

Kendall rolled off the couch, tugging her skirt down over her hips and buttoning her shirt. "I made this one a long time ago. It's a promise I have to keep."

The big cowboy pulled on his shorts, then crossed his arms over his chest. "Don't go."

Kendall's stomach fluttered. The look in Ed's eyes was everything she could have hoped for. But was she afraid of reading more than what was really there? "Cory is counting on me."

Ed's hands dropped to his sides, his fists clenching. "Cory's the dude I met earlier? The one you've had over at your place every day when I come home?"

"That's him." Kendall leaned up on her toes and pressed a kiss to Ed's tight lips. "Thanks for the lesson. Same time tomorrow?"

His jaw tightened. "We'll see."

Kendall frowned, all joy of having made love to Ed leeching away. "Did I say something to make you mad?"

He shook his head then he grabbed her arms and stared down at her. "Don't let some jerk take advantage of you."

"What if I want him to?" Kendall teased.

Instead of laughing, Ed's frown deepened.

"Kendall?" Lacey called out.

"I'm coming," Kendall yelled. Turning back to him, she sighed. "We need to talk."

"Let's talk now."

"I can't." She turned for the door, stopping with her hand on the knob. "But we will talk." Then she left, shutting the door behind her before she could change her mind.

"I was about to give up and go without you." Lacey stood at the front door to the big old house. Her face split in a grin. "You did it, didn't you?"

Kendall sucked in a deep breath and let it out slowly. "Yes."

"And?"

A tear slipped out of the corner of her eyes.

"That good, huh?" Lacey shook her head. "Damn."

"Better. I didn't want to leave." She glanced over her shoulder at Ed's door.

"Don't do it, Kendall. He thinks you have a date. You didn't tell him the lessons were to land him, did you?"

Her throat clogged with dryness. "No, but I need to."

"Did he tell you he loves you?"

Kendall frowned. "No. But he's just getting used to the idea of making love to his best friend's little sister. I should tell him how I feel about him." Butterflies flickered in her belly. She started to turn back toward Ed's apartment.

Lacey grabbed her hand. "Not yet. You have to go through with this 'date' with Cory to see if Ed's jealous enough to come after you."

"But it's not a date and, telling Ed it is, is lying to him."

"He'll survive. And won't Plan B be worth the effort if it pushes him over the edge and makes him come to his senses?"

"What if he doesn't?" Kendall pulled free of Lacey's hand. "What if all of this was a waste of time? What if Ed doesn't love me like that?" Her shoulders slumped.

"Did you two make love?"

Kendall smiled, her eyes filling. She nodded, her throat too clogged with tears to choke out words.

"Baby, he had to love you if he'd do it with Connor's little sister."

A shoulder lifted in a shrug. "He thinks I'd go to

Whitey Ross for lessons. He didn't have much of a choice."

"The man had choices. Trust me." Lacey turned Kendall toward the stairs. "Now run up and throw on a bra and panties. Going without underwear with Ed is one thing, but at the Ugly Stick Saloon, you'll start a riot."

"It's Ladies' Night."

Lacey nodded, her eyes wide. "I know. Some of those so-called ladies are horny enough to jump a cute little thing like you, given enough provocation. Without a bra and panties, you're definitely provoking." She slapped Kendall's ass with enough oomph to send her racing up the stairs.

As soon as Cory did his dance, Kendall would head home and pick up where she and Ed had left off.

She hoped.

ED PACED the floor of his apartment once, twice, three times before he gave up.

Footsteps echoed through the ceiling from Kendall's apartment above him. She was probably getting ready for her date.

Anger surged through Ed. How could she go on a date after they'd made love only a few minutes ago? He spun and resumed the pacing.

Was she really in love with someone else? Were the sex lessons just that? Lessons? How could she let him do the things she did without feeling some kind of connection?

Ed sure as hell had felt a connection. Kendall Mason had rocked his world, making him see her for the first time as a fully-grown, very sexy woman. One he wanted in his bed for more than just lessons in sex lessons she'd use on another man.

Her footsteps crossed the floor above and a door opened and closed.

Damn, she was going out and he could do nothing.

Or couldn't he?

Ed raced into his bedroom, pulled on jeans over his shorts, jammed his feet into his cowboy boots and grabbed a shirt as he ran out the door. He'd follow her on her date. If Cory tried anything, damn it...well, he'd cross that bridge when he slammed into it.

Kendall's car sat in the driveway. Cory must have taken her in his topless sports car.

Ed growled. Damned sports cars didn't provide any protection in a rollover. Convertibles were too dangerous and the people who drove them tended to drive too fast. Ed would never take the woman he loved out in a convertible. No sirree.

Holy Hell. His boots skidded on the sidewalk.

Had he just thought the L-word?

CHAPTER EIGHT

*E*d jumped in his truck and revved the engine, spinning gravel as he pulled out of the driveway onto the road. If he hoped to catch up with Kendall, he'd have to hurry. When he slowed for a stop sign, all he saw was Lacey's car, turning at the end of the next block. No sign of Cory's convertible.

Maybe Lacey knew where Kendall was headed. He turned where Lacey had turned and gunned the accelerator. Lacey had a heavy foot and tended to break speed limits.

Ed tried to catch her but managed to get behind a Grandma Moses, going twenty in a forty zone. Far ahead, Lacey turned west on the main road headed out of town. Ed realized she was headed for the Ugly Stick Saloon where she worked as a waitress. By the time Ed pulled into the parking lot, Lacey had rounded the back of the building and parked. He'd missed her going into the bar.

Cars and pickup trucks filled the parking lot loaded with females, all laughing, smiling and headed for the door. What was the deal? Where were the men?

Ed dropped down out of his truck, jammed his hat on his head and ran for the door, still buttoning his shirt. "Excuse me, excuse me." As he eased his way through the mob, the woman laughed, whistled at him and ran their hands over his chest and butt.

"Are you the talent?" one asked.

"I'd stuff his G-string with every bill in my wallet."

"Hell, I'd give him my credit card."

"Hey, cowboy, I got a twenty with our name on it."

Ed smiled and laughed it off, feeling like chum thrown into a shark-feeding frenzy. When he reached the door, Big Joe Sealy blocked the entrance. "Sorry, Ed, it's ladies night. No men allowed."

"What?" Ed tried to look past Joe in hope of getting Lacey's attention, but the man completely blocked his view. "I'm not staying. I just need to talk to Lacey."

"That's right, you ain't stayin'." Joe crossed his burly arms. "No men past this point. I got strict orders, only ladies are allowed in. The male talent enters through the rear entrance. If you ain't male talent, you ain't gettin' in."

The man was as loyal and as trustworthy as they come, even if he wasn't the sharpest tool in the shed. "What if I told you it was an emergency?"

"Dial 9-1-1. Now git." Joe jerked his head and let several women through.

His fists clenching, Ed turned and waded through the sea of females. He got pinched twice and one stuffed a dollar into the waistband of his jeans. At this rate, he'd never catch up with Kendall.

When he'd almost cleared the line, a bleach-blonde, forty-something woman wreaking of alcohol threw her arms around him. "Are you the talent? Cause I'm callin' dibs."

He smiled down at her and untangled her arms from around his neck. "Sorry, lady. I'm taken." As soon as he made it past the crowd, he headed for the truck.

A convertible screamed into the parking lot and almost clipped him. Without slowing, it headed straight for the back of the saloon.

The pretty blond boy in the driver's seat had to be Cory. But where was Kendall? Had she come with Lacey?

Fuck. Ed rounded the side of the building and jogged to the rear. He was just in time to see Cory enter through the back door. Was that scrawny little twerp the talent? And what kind of date involved Kendall providing her own transportation? A real man came to the lady's front door and escorted her to his truck. He didn't arrange to meet her at some bar.

Shaking his head, he marched for the back

entrance, ready to give Kendall and Cory a piece of his mind. As he reached for the doorknob, it jerked open.

"Oh, thank goodness. You must be the new guy. You're late." A woman with ham fists that put Big Joe Sealy's to shame, grabbed his arm and pulled him through the door. "Your costume's hanging in the changing room. It's the leather chaps and whip. If you don't have your own G-string, there's a spare on the shelf at the rear of the room. Move it, you're on in five minutes."

She gave him a hefty shove, sending him into a room crowded with pumped up, mostly naked men.

A man dressed in what might once have been a policeman's uniform hurried by. "Dude, you better hurry. The natives are restless and we're on in four minutes." As he passed, Ed noted the back of his trousers had been cut out, displaying a shocking amount of man-ass.

When Ed didn't respond, the guy looked over his shoulder. "You are Fred's fill-in, aren't you? If not, you can't be in here. It's ladies night and no men are allowed in the saloon except the talent."

Ed gulped and made his decision. "Guess that makes me the talent." He forced a smile and hurriedly added, "Are there some chaps around here? I hear that's my costume."

"On the hook over there." The cop nodded to the rear of the room.

By now, most of the men had slipped into skimpy

costumes, rubbed oil on their perfectly tanned torsos and strutted to the edge of the curtain.

"Chop, chop!" The woman from the back door stepped inside and clapped her hands. She handed him a black mask. "Tonight, you're the lone ranger. Go get 'em, cowboy."

Ed stripped and grabbed a package labeled G-string. Never in all his life had he ever planned on wearing what he had always referred to as butt floss. Tonight was the exception. He packed his jewels into the triangle of material which unfortunately barely concealed half of his length. And damned if the thought of all those women out there didn't make the fit twice as bad. His cock swelled, stretching the material away from his body.

Holy Hell.

"We're on!" someone shouted.

Ed tied the chaps around his waist and the mask around his head. At least he'd be able to check on Kendall without her suspecting a thing. The music rose in a highly suggestive bump-and-grind tune. The crowd of women screamed, the cacophony drowning out the music.

His heart hammering in his chest, Ed stepped out onto a brightly lit stage, temporarily blinded by the lights pointed up at the performers.

The cop leaned over and yelled in Ed's ear, "Dance, man, dance. They tip better if you shake it in their faces."

Ed edged out onto the stage, careful to keep from

turning around. His ass was cold and he didn't want to moon the women gathered for the show.

Holy Hell. What had he gotten himself into?

KENDALL SAT at the edge of the stage, Lacey next her to drinking a light beer, hootin' and hollerin' like she hadn't seen this a dozen times before.

"There he is." Kendall smiled and waved at Cory.

He danced his way over to Kendall and shook his hips, twisting and gyrating the way Kendall had taught him. Cory had natural rhythm. All Kendall had done was shown him a few moves that would get attention and hopefully land him extra tips to help him with the rent while he attended college.

Kendall was so proud of him. He had a great body, why not make enough cash in one night to pay the rent for the next two months? That way, his studies didn't have to suffer by holding down a full-time job and going to school at night.

Cory reached down his hand.

Kendall had a dollar ready to slap into his palm.

Only he didn't take the money, he pulled her up onto the stage with a quick tug.

"What are you doing?" She laughed and tried to step down.

"Rather than one of those other horny women. Please help me with the show and save me from the masses. You're good at this." He danced around her, grinding his pelvis into her hips.

Kendall's cheeks burned. If Cory was more comfortable by dancing the first song with her, what could it hurt? She smiled and laughed, pretending to be one of the random women the men selected on occasion to fuel the crowd.

Cory twirled her around and backed her into his arms, his cock grinding against her ass, his hands sliding down her sides to her hips.

It was yet another one of the moves Kendall had taught him, and he was doing so well. Kendall should have moved off the stage and let him bring another woman up onto stage. One with money burning a hole in her pocket.

Kendall straightened, laughing. "You're on your own, Cory."

Cory jerked away and a larger pair of hands clamped around her waist, holding her in place. "What the hell?" When she twisted toward her captor, he refused to let her, his hips pumping to the rhythm of the music, his hands sliding up her waist.

Cory danced by with a shrug and a grin.

Kendall's heart raced, defensive instincts kicking in. "Let go of me."

Chaps flapped against her legs. Chaps that barely covered the massive thighs beneath them.

Kendall's heart raced and a slow burn skimmed beneath every inch of her skin. A quick glance over her shoulder did nothing to quell the rise of heat in her body. The man behind her wore a cowboy hat and a black mask. "Who are you?"

The man's mouth curved upward in a deadly sexy smile. "The Lone Ranger, ma'am. Here to rescue you," he said in a deep voice.

So deep, Kendall could have fallen into it. Her breath grew ragged as the cowboy's hands slid up from her waist to cup her breasts. Kendall leaned back into him, his tough leather and man-musk scent making her knees weak. "No, really." Her voice ragged, she swallowed hard and continued. "Who are you?"

"Ride with me into the sunset, beautiful lady, and I'll reveal all."

Her heart skipped several beats then raced to catch up. Hell, what was she thinking? She loved Ed, not this sexy cowboy who danced in strip clubs. "No. No, I can't. I have a boyfriend. I'm practically engaged."

He spun her away from him and back into his arms so that she faced him. "This Cory dude is not the man for you."

Her boobs crashed into his naked chest, forcing her breath out in a gasp. Kendall stared into the man's sky blue eyes.

He lifted his cowboy hat and winked.

"Ed?" Joy swelled in her chest as Kendall stood stock still in the middle of the dance floor. "What are you doing here?"

"Keeping you from making a mistake with pretty boy." He nodded his head toward Cory.

"By dancing naked in front of all these barracudas?" She shook her head and laughed out loud. "Really, why are you here?"

"That's just it. I couldn't let you go out on a date with Cory. He's not the right man for you."

Irritation straightened her spine. Kendall planted her fists on her hips and faced off with Ed Judson. "No? Then who is, Ed? Who is the right man for me?"

Ed opened his mouth to answer, but before any words could come out, Big Joe Sealy plucked Kendall from the stage and set her on the barroom floor. "Time's up, Kendall. Let one of the other ladies have a shot at the cowboy."

"But, Joe, I need to be up there." Kendall placed her hands on the wooden surface and tried to climb back up.

Big Joe planted a heavy hand on her shoulder. With the other hand, he helped a forty-something bleach blonde climb onto the stage where she immediately flung herself into Ed's arms.

A surge of jealousy ripped through Kendall's gut.

Ed peeled the woman's death grip from around his neck, and he spun her away from him and back.

His moves were not nearly as practiced or suggestive as the other strippers, but still fun to watch. When he turned his back to the audience, Kendall gasped and clapped a hand to her mouth.

Ed's very tight, very manly ass shone like a neon moon.

Women roared and surged toward the stage, bills clenched in their fists or hanging from their teeth. They shoved Kendall out of the way, pushing her farther and farther away from the cowboy and his gorgeous tush.

The blonde in Ed's arms pulled her top over her head and flung it out into the crowd. Wearing nothing but a black demi-bra, the woman jumped up and wrapped her legs around Ed's waist, pressing her D cups into his face. She yanked his hat off his head and waved it in the air, shouting, "Ride me, cowboy!"

Ed's eyes widened and he looked out into the crowd. When he caught a glimpse of Kendall, he mouthed the word, *help.*

Kendall crossed her arms over her chest and shook her head. "You're on your own." If Ed had hoped to stop her from seeing Cory, he deserved to be caught in his little act by all these women. Let him suffer. If he hoped to win her heart, his answers had to be faster and he had to be fully prepared to declare his love. He needed to see what a treasure he had in Kendall and that having all the women in the world was not the right answer for him.

The song faded out and a roar of applause sure to deafen every ear in the room rose to a crescendo. The men made a final pass along the edge of the stage, allowing women to stuff their G-strings with bills, then they escaped behind the curtain.

Big Joe Sealy had to untangle the blonde from Ed before he could beat a retreat.

Finally backstage, Ed sucked in a deep breath and let it out slowly.

"Not used to the meat market, are you?" The cop slapped him on the back and grinned. "Don't worry, after the first dance, you just go with the flow."

Flow, hell. Ed didn't plan on dancing another dance in front of those rabid women. All he wanted was get into his jeans and shirt, find Kendall and get her the hell out of there.

"Hey, cowboy, nice ass." A hand slapped his butt, staying there a little longer than necessary.

Ed spun, ready to defend his honor and politely tell the woman he was done playing stripper.

Lacey leaned against the wall, her lips twisted, her brows waggling. "You looked damn fine out there tonight."

"Don't get used to it."

She tipped her head, her gaze going to the flesh exposed by chaps way too small for his thick thighs. "I don't know. I think you can make a killing with that equipment.

Heat crawled across his chest and Ed covered his package with cupped hands. "Cut it out."

"So, why'd you come?"

"Would you believe I wanted to try my hand at stripping?"

Lacey shook her head. "Try again."

At just that moment, Cory entered the dressing room.

Ed straightened. "I came to talk Kendall out of

dating that gigolo." His fists clenched. "Maybe I should just have a word with the man, instead of Kendall."

Lacey placed a hand in the middle of Ed's chest, stopping him before he could take a step. "Wrong."

"What do you mean wrong?" Ed heaved a ragged sigh.

"Cory's not the problem."

"Then who the hell is?" Ed raised both fists. "I'll kill him."

Lacey grinned. "You."

"Me?" His hands unclenched and jammed onto his waist.

"Yeah, big guy." Her hand fell to her side. "Why do you think Kendall was willing to let you teach her sex education lessons?"

"Because she trusts me?" Surely, that was the reason that made the most sense.

Lacey snorted and shook her head.

Ed's brows furrowed. "I couldn't let her go to Whitey Ross for lessons."

"Kendall needs lessons about sex like an alcoholic needs to learn how to drink. She gave up her virginity when she was eighteen."

His chest squeezed tight. "I'd like to punch the kid that took it."

"Why?"

"Because. She was just a kid."

"And why don't you want her to date Cory?"

Lacey nodded toward the blond pretty boy. "Kendall's not a kid anymore."

"I promised Connor I'd look out for her." But damn, the girl had grown into a beautiful woman.

"What if she loves Cory?"

"I'll kill him." Blood thundered in his ears.

"Why?" Lacey looked him directly in the eye.

"Because I love her." Ed gripped Lacey's arms. "I love Kendall. Are you happy? I love my best friend's little sister."

Lacey's face split into a wide grin. "Honey, you'll have to get over that one, if you really love her and want to be with her."

Ed glanced over at Cory. "What about the pretty face over there?"

"She's been teaching him how to dance. That's all."

"To dance?" He stared from Cory back to Lacey, his head swimming with the possibility that he might have a chance with Kendall. "I thought she wanted the lessons to get a guy to notice her."

"It worked, didn't it?" Her lips spread into a wide grin. "You noticed her, didn't you?"

"You're kidding right? All that sex education bull-shit was to get my attention?" Ed shook his head. He turned and walked a few steps away, oblivious to the draft on his backside, then spun and returned to Lacey. "Why didn't she just tell me?"

Lacey's cheeks reddened. "I kinda talked her into the whole Sex Ed plan."

"You?" Ed ran his hand through his hair.

"Yeah. I figured it would give her one more chance to get your attention."

"Before what?"

"Before she moved to Austin and started over."

All the air whooshed out of Ed's lungs. He had never considered Kendall might move away. If he was honest with himself, he suspected his reluctance toward building his own house had a lot to do with Kendall sharing the one he lived in. "She was right. I refused to look at her as anything other than Connor's sister."

Lacey's brows rose, a smile quirking the edges of her lips. "Yeah, but you never brought women back to your apartment."

"I couldn't." He laughed. "Bringing another woman into the same house didn't feel right."

"And you haven't married any of the women you've dated."

"Again, it just didn't feel right."

"Now that you've been with Kendall?"

Ed grinned. "She feels right." He slapped his hat on his leg. "Damn it, it feels so right I want to tell her."

Lacey frowned. "Tell her what? That it feels right?" She shook her head. "It'll take more than that to win that girl over. The big question is, do you love her?"

Ed's grin grew even wider. "Yes, ma'am. More than anything."

"Even more than disappointing your friend?"

Ed sobered. "I need to talk to Connor before I do anything."

"The sooner, the better." A smile lit Lacey's face. "You're going to marry her, aren't you?"

"Damn straight. Before she gets anymore cocka-mamie ideas about sex education."

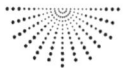

CHAPTER NINE

Kendall pushed her way through the crowd, angling for the door to the dressing room backstage. Ed's punishment with the other women had gone on quite long enough. If Ed had come to 'rescue' her from Cory, Kendall hoped he acted because he was jealous, not just doing his brotherly-duty. Perhaps the Cory baiting had done the trick and made him realize he had a little competition, and that he'd better speak up or shut up.

Her efforts to get to the dressing room became more forceful, until she soon shoved women out of the way. What if he'd been about to declare his love when Big Joe yanked Kendall off the stage?

Ed might really be in love with her and she wanted to know now.

When she reached the dressing room, she waited until the security guard left his post for a moment to answer a question of one of the bar patrons.

Kendall ran, grabbed the door knob and jerked it open. Once inside, she slammed the door closed behind her. Another song started, and the crowd of women screamed so loud, no amount of wall insulation could muffle the cries. Several of the men had changed costumes and were headed back to the stage. One by one, the crowd of men in the dressing area thinned until Kendall finally spotted Ed on the opposite end of the room.

He had his back to her, still wearing the chaps that exposed his really fine ass in the G-string.

Kendall's steps picked up and she almost laughed out loud. She couldn't wait until she could pinch him. She had a smart-ass remark poised on her lips, ready for when he spotted her.

Ed turned to the side, his body in silhouette even more powerful and beautiful in Kendall's eyes. He smiled and laughed at someone standing in the shadows.

Then a slim pair of arms wrapped around his neck and a woman with auburn hair flung herself at him, kissing him full on the lips.

Lacey.

Kendall's feet ground to a halt and she backed behind a stage prop, her little bubble of happiness exploding deep in her chest. How could she have been so wrong? Ed looked so happy, like a man in love. In love with Lacey, not her.

Audrey Anderson, the owner of the saloon passed

in front of her, stopped and returned. "Kendall? You're not supposed to be in here."

"It's okay, I'm leaving." Kendall spoke softly. She didn't want Ed and Lacey to find her there. If they said anything to her right then, she was likely to fall completely apart. "I just wanted to congratulate Cory on a great performance." She turned away from the sight of Ed and Lacey hugging and kissing, her heart so heavy she could barely breathe.

"Audrey," a voice called out from the storeroom.

Audrey glanced back at her bartender waving, trying to get her attention. "Coming." She frowned at Kendall. "Sweetheart, you don't look well. Do you want me to have someone give you a ride home?" Audrey touched her arm.

"Audrey!"

Kendall forced a smile. "I'm fine. I can get myself home. But, thanks."

Audrey gave her one last look and hurried toward the storeroom.

Cory from the prop room. "Oh, Kendall, I'm so glad I caught you." He hugged her close and then pushed back, grinning. "Thanks for your help. I made enough in tips to pay for three months' rent on my apartment. If you hadn't taught me how to dance, I don't know how I'd have managed. Those women are crazy." He laughed and hugged her, again. "I better get back out there. There's more money to be made while it lasts."

"You go. I'm headed out the back door."

"Are you okay?" Cory stared into her face, a frown pulling his brows low.

"I'm fine." She waved a hand in front of her neck. "I just need air. Crowds, you know."

"Yeah, I know. Especially this one." He grinned. "Thanks again." He disappeared through the curtain, leaving Kendall to find her way out without alerting Lacey and Ed to her presence.

One of the dancers carried a large Mexican sombrero to the props shelf.

Kendall ducked behind the hat and walked with him until she could peel off and head for the rear door. Without looking back, she pushed through the door. As soon as the cool night air hit her burning cheeks, the tears fell.

Had that been Lacey's plan all along? Had she insinuated herself into the Sex Ed lessons because Ed was getting too close to Kendall and she wanted Ed for herself?

A lead weight settled in Kendall's gut. Maybe Ed had been playing her all along. Maybe he'd always loved Lacey and Kendall hadn't seen it. Had the two of them been in cahoots all along, waiting for Kendall to give up and move on?

Kendall's feet carried her through the parking lot, one slow, heavy step at a time.

A cop car cruised through, moving just as slowly.

Kendall dodged his cruiser and hit the highway, her pace increasing.

The cop pulled alongside. "Lady, you need a ride home?"

Kendall kept her head averted, not one to cry in front of strangers. "No." She needed to walk out her frustrations or at least until her tears dried. Given what she'd just witnessed, that might be a very long walk.

"It's supposed to start raining," the cop said. "I don't feel right leaving you out here walking alone."

"I don't need a ride." She sniffed and scrubbed a hand across her face.

"Suit yourself." He slowed his police vehicle to a stop.

Kendall kept walking toward town. Five miles. The distance was only five miles from the saloon to the house. She could jog that in her sleep.

A fat drop of rain landed square between her eyes and dripped down over her nose. Another fell, then another, mixing with the tears. Soon the heavens opened and dumped on Kendall. She couldn't see to walk and every step landed in another dark rut filled with water. "Why?" she yelled to the sky. "Why?"

The cop car pulled up, his windshield wipers flinging even more water onto her. "Get in." Door locks clicked.

Kendall yanked open the front passenger door and got in, completely soaked and past caring. She gave the police officer her address and closed her eyes for the remainder of the short ride, determined to avoid conversation. Even if she tried, she couldn't speak past the wad of tears clogging her throat.

As they pulled in front of the house, the cop shifted into park and turned toward her. "He's not worth it. A guy who'd let you go isn't worth the trouble." He held up his hands. "Just saying."

"Thanks for the ride." Kendall got out, closed the door and trudged up the steps to her apartment.

The cop had it right. The man wasn't worth it.

If that was the case, then why was she so broken hearted?

ED DRESSED in the jeans and shirt he'd worn into the building and peeked around the curtain, looking for Kendall. Lacey had gone out into the crowd to find her while Ed changed.

He spotted Lacey, but no Kendall.

Lacey waved at him from across the floor and jerked her head toward the exit.

They met outside at the rear of the building. Big fat raindrops fell from the sky at random.

"Did she leave?" Ed asked.

Lacey shrugged. "I looked in the bathroom and everywhere else I could think of. She's not in the saloon."

Ed's pulse quickened. "You don't think she's in trouble, do you?"

"She rode with me." Lacey frowned.

"I'm worried something's happened."

"Let me check with Cory. Maybe he's seen her." Lacey ducked back inside the back door.

As Ed paced the parking lot, the rain let loose, dumping down on him. He headed for the door to see what was keeping Lacey and reached for the doorknob.

Lacey emerged, her face pale. "Cory said Kendall was in the dressing room a few minutes ago and said she was going out the back for some air. I looked again and didn't see any sign of her anywhere."

Before Lacey finished speaking, Ed ran for his truck, his boots splashing in the puddles. "I'm headed to the house."

"I'll see you there," Lacey called out behind him.

Ed ran around to the front of the Ugly Stick Saloon and leaped into his truck, shaking the water out of his hair. Where the hell was Kendall? If she'd been in the dressing room, why hadn't she told him or Lacey that she was leaving?

All the worst-case scenarios sprang to mind. An image sprang to mind of Kendall stepping out back for a breath of air and being grabbed by some ape of a man, thrown into his car and taken into some back-woods area where he'd rape and murder her.

Anger stiffened his muscles. Ed's boot hit the accelerator hard, spitting gravel up behind him. His truck skidded sideways onto the slick highway, straightened and sped toward the house.

He couldn't let his imagination take over. Everything would be okay. A logical explanation existed for Kendall's disappearance. She probably got a ride home with someone and left a message with one of the wait staff who forgot to deliver it.

Holy Hell. Was it five miles or fifteen to his house?

His cell phone rang in his pocket and he almost had a wreck answering it. "Kendall?"

"No, it's me, Connor. Is something wrong?"

Ed wanted to shout *Yes!* But he couldn't upset his friend, not while he couldn't do anything to help. "No, nothing." He prayed.

"Why did you think I was Kendall?"

"Look, Connor, I'm in a hurry, and there's no good way to do this other than to jump in." Bracing his hands on the wheel, Ed took a deep breath and announced, "I love your sister and want to marry her."

"Holy smokes, Ed," Connor yelled into the phone. "I thought you were fixin' to give me bad news. Don't scare me like that."

Ed's foot eased up on the accelerator. "What, you're not upset or disappointed?"

"Are you kidding? About time you two got together. Kendall's been in love with you since forever."

"Why was I the last to know it?"

"Hey, I'm your friend. I wasn't going to push my kid sister at you. Besides, she had some growing up to do."

Ed's thoughts went back to banana pudding and whipped cream. "Oh, she's all grown up now."

"Yeah. Why do you think I asked you to keep an eye on her? I hoped you'd wake up to that fact."

Ed shook his head and slammed his foot on the brake. "Look, Connor, I'm driving in the rain to get to Kendall and ask her to marry me. On your next call to her, ask her what her answer is."

"Will do. And congrats."

Tossing his cell phone in the seat beside him, Ed prayed Kendall was at home and safe so that he could propose. He took all the corners too fast, hydroplaning sideways, almost clipping two stop signs. By the time he reached the house, his heart was pounding so hard, he thought it would jump right out of his chest.

Ed drove the pickup into the drive, slammed it into park and jumped out, leaving the engine running, the keys in the ignition. If Kendall wasn't home, he didn't know where he'd look, but he'd look until he found her. *Damn it, she'd better be home.*

With long strides, he took the steps two at a time. When he reached her apartment door, he banged it hard with his fists. "Kendall!" He continued banging in case she was in the shower or blow-drying her hair. She had to hear him. She had to be there.

Scared out of his wits, he backed up, ready to throw himself at the door and break it down, when the door suddenly opened.

Kendall stood there, wrapped in nothing but a towel, her eyes wide and red-rimmed, her hair dripping down around her shoulders. "Ed? Where's the fire?"

"Holy Hell." He enveloped her in his arms and hugged her so fiercely, she squeaked.

"What's wrong with you?" Kendall pushed against him.

"Is she here?" Lacey's footsteps echoed on the stairs behind Ed.

"She's here." Ed still held Kendall in his arms, even as she pushed to free herself.

"Of course, I'm here. Where else would I be?"

"In a ditch, murdered, raped, dead." Ed yanked her against his body again and held her there. "Don't ever scare me like that again."

"I'm not dead, or raped, or murdered. I just came home. Now let me go." Her hands planted firmly against his chest and she pushed so hard, Ed was forced to let go. "You left without telling anyone." Ed ran a hand through his wet hair, dragging in a deep breath. "What was I supposed to think?"

Kendall stepped away, her head averted, refusing to meet his gaze. "Ed, you're not my keeper. Whatever you promised my brother is bullshit. I'm not your responsibility."

"To hell with your brother." His hand pounded his chest. "What about me? What if I care enough to know where you are?"

"You won't have to worry about me much longer." Her chin jutted out, her bottom lip trembling. "After I graduate from college next month, I'm headed to

Austin. Out of sight will be out of mind. You and Lacey can carry on without me in the way." She grabbed the edge of the door and tried to close it. "Now if you'll excuse me, I'm going to bed."

"Me and Lacey?" Ed looked at her, sure she'd lost her mind. "What do you mean, me and Lacey?"

Lacey stepped up beside Ed. "Kendall, what are you talking about?"

Kendall's eyes pooled and a dammed tear slipped out and trailed down her cheek. Hadn't she cried enough? "I thought you were my friend."

Lacey's brows drew together and she pushed past Ed, reaching out to take Kendall in her arms. "I *am* your friend."

Kendall held up her hands, backing away from Lacey. "No. How can you be when you came up with this whole Sex Ed plan? All along you wanted Ed for yourself."

Lacey's frown deepened. "Me, want Ed? No way. He's yours."

"I'm not at all into Lacey." Ed shook his head. "Where did you get an idea like that?"

"You don't have to hide it anymore." Kendall swiped at the tears streaming down her face and tipped up her chin. "I saw you two kissing in the dressing room at the Ugly Stick."

Lacey's brows rose, her eyes rounding. "You saw me kissing Ed because I was happy for him. Not because I love him. The kiss was sisterly, nothing more."

"Yeah, and I'm just a naive college girl, gullible and easily tricked. No thanks. You two can have each other." With a heavy heart, Kendall tried again to shut the door.

"Kendall, I'd just told Lacey that I love you. She was so excited that she kissed me. The kiss didn't mean anything. I love *you*." Ed pushed the door wider and made a grab for Kendall's arm.

Joy dared to spring into her heart, but she wouldn't let herself be hurt again. She dodged him and moved farther back into the apartment. "No, you just feel responsible for me because of some dumb promise you made to my brother."

"I love you. And not because of the promise I made to your brother." He followed her into the apartment, his steps slow, measured, like an animal stalking his prey. "I think I've always loved you. It took some crazy female plan to make me see it."

Kendall backed up a step further until her bottom ran into the sofa. "I don't believe you," she whispered.

"Then let me tell you again." His hands slid up her arms and rounded to the back of her neck, tipping her head back. "I love you, Kendall Mason."

"Uh, I'll just let myself out. Maybe I'll just go turn off your truck and collect the keys." Lacey chuckled. "You two can handle things from here." The door to Kendall's apartment closed with a soft snick.

Kendall couldn't tear her gaze away from Ed's, his blue eyes burned into her, swarms of butterflies attacking her insides. "You love me?"

"Yup." He bent to brush a kiss across her lips. "I just needed a little sex education to show me how much."

"What about my brother?" Kendall leaned into Ed, her lips pressing into his.

Ed reached into his pocket and pulled out his cell phone. "Connor called me on the way to the house. He's on board and told me to plan the wedding for when he's back and can give you away proper."

"He did?" Her eyes widened and a huge swell of happiness filled her. "I love you, Ed Judson. I've loved you my entire life."

"Then why the hell did you wait so long to tell me?" He gathered her against him, his mouth slanting across hers, his tongue thrusting between her teeth.

The kiss sparked a fire inside Kendall that burned away the cold of the drenching rain and mistaken betrayal. She let go of the edge of her towel, letting it fall to the floor. "I'm ready for my next lesson," she said against his mouth.

Ed laughed out loud, scooped her up in his arms and carried her into the bedroom. "I have a feeling you could teach *me* a few things." He laid her on the bed and stripped his damp shirt from his shoulders.

"Maybe." With a wicked grin, Kendall eased open the buttons on his jeans and pushed them down over his hips. "Shall we start here?" His cock sprang free into her hands.

With slow, steady strokes, she slid her hands up

and down his length, reveling in the smooth skin encasing hardened steel. He was hers. All hers.

Kendall took him into her mouth, grabbing around his hips to pull him deeper until his cock bumped against the back of her throat. His dick filled her mouth, stretching her lips.

His hands threaded into her hair as he thrust in and out, faster and faster. When his body stiffened, he pulled free and climbed on the bed with her, parting her knees.

Kendall stared up into his eyes as he drove into her body, burying his cock deep, filling her, stretching her channel in the most delicious way. Her heels dug into the sheets, pushing her up to meet him, thrust for thrust. Never in her life had she felt this complete, this loved and cherished by a man. Her body tensed, the tingling beginning at her core and spreading outward to the tips of her fingers. Kendall cried out his name as she burst over the edge. "Ed."

Ed held her hips as he plunged in one last time, his cock pulsing inside her, his fingers digging into her skin. Then he collapsed on top of her and rolled them to the side, without severing their intimate connection. "You aren't the little girl I used to know."

"Is that a bad thing?" Kendall smoothed the lock of hair off his forehead, loving that they lay naked in her bed, their bodies joined.

"Oh, it's very bad, in a very good way." He kissed her and thrust into her again.

The cell phone on Kendall's bedside table rang, vibrating so much it rattled across the wood surface.

Kendall frowned and reached to turn it off when she saw the caller id flashing *Connor Mason*. She glanced at Ed. "It's Connor."

He nodded, leaning in to nibble at her throat. "Answer."

With a smile, Kendall draped a leg over Ed's hip and poked the Talk button. "Hi, brother. How's the war?"

"Forget the war, I hear congratulations are in order. My baby sister is engaged."

Kendall frowned at the phone. "What?"

A long pause then, "Oops, did I jump the gun?"

Ed took the phone from Kendall. "I was just getting to that. Thanks, buddy." He handed back the phone.

As Kendall pressed it to her ear, Ed thrust into her.

"Will you marry me, Kendall Mason?"

"Say yes!" Connor shouted into her ear.

Kendall sucked in a deep breath and held it, the feeling of Ed hard and thick deep inside her threatening to steal the air from her lungs. "Yes," she said, all the air rushing out of her lungs at once. "Yes, Ed Judson. I'll marry you." Into the phone, she said, "Gotta go, Connor. We're celebrating our engagement."

"Hey, no babies until I can give you away at the wedding."

"I'm making no promises." Kendall clicked the disconnect button and switched off the phone. "Now, where were we?" Her arms curled around Ed's neck and she drew him down for a long kiss. "Ah yes. You were about to give me the next installment of Sex Ed."

Enjoy other Ugly Stick Saloon books by Myla Jackson

BOOTS & LEATHER

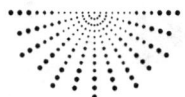

UGLY STICK SALOON SERIES BOOK #3

New York Times & USA Today
Bestselling Author
ELLE JAMES

writing as

MYLA JACKSON

BOOTS & LEATHER

UGLY STICK SALOON

New York Times Bestselling Author

ELLE JAMES

writing as

MYLA JACKSON

*L*ibby Jones flipped the whiskey bottle in the air and caught it without spilling a drop, then poured a round of shots for the two men who'd pulled up a stool at the bar. She filled two mugs with beer from the tap and slapped them on the counter. "Anything else I can do for you boys?"

"How's about a lap dance, beautiful?" one suggested, grinning. His smile displayed two missing front teeth.

The man beside him elbowed him in the gut. "What would yer wife say, Harmon?"

Harmon shrugged. "She'd probably tell me to take out the trash."

"Yeah, meaning you. Then she'd knock the rest of those teeth out of that stupid head of yers."

"Shut up, Reggie." Harmon frowned. "Got those teeth knocked out ridin' a bull on the circuit."

"That bull bein' the husband of that ugly redhead

in Amarillo." Reggie slapped a hand on Harmon's back and roared with laughter. "Wasn't worth it, was it?"

Libby sighed. The same old drunks with the same stories always managed to end up at her barstools. Where were all the good-looking cowboys tonight? She glanced across the crowded saloon. That's where they were. On the dance floor, while she was serving drinks behind the bar.

The Gray Wolf twins, Mark and Luke, spun around for the umpteenth time, laughing and smiling, making every girl in the place drool.

Even me. Libby sighed again. Back in her other life, she'd be the one dancing and someone else would be serving her drinks. But then, she'd hated her other life. No. Libby was better off tending bar and keeping to herself than playing the pampered princess in a city full of people. At least in Temptation, Texas, she could get away from the noise and crowds when she wanted.

Audrey Anderson, the owner of the Ugly Stick Saloon, laid a hand on Libby's shoulder. "'Bout ready for your break?"

"Past ready." Libby pulled the towel off her shoulder and tossed it on the bar. "I'll be out back."

"The cowboys 'round here can get pretty rowdy," Audrey warned. "You sure you'll be all right?"

"Better than being inside all night." Libby burst through the back door of the saloon into the night, sucking in a deep breath of fresh air that didn't reek of alcohol and sweaty men.

Eight months she'd been working at the Ugly Stick Saloon. Longer than anywhere else she'd stayed over the past couple years. Eight months she'd been watching others having fun and partying, flirting with the handsome cowboys, two of whom had definitely caught her eye since she'd started working at the saloon. Libby's shoulders tensed. She was better off forgetting about flirting with the Gray Wolf men. A low profile had been her goal for the past two years and the only thing that kept her out of trouble.

Still, she had yearnings...needs...a hunger for something more.

Perhaps it was time to move on.

The door behind her opened and closed, footsteps crunching in the gravel toward her.

She walked faster, craving the quiet time alone. Before she'd gone two yards, the footsteps caught up with her and hands slid down her shoulders.

"Hey, beautiful. Need a ride home?" A big, smelly man with bad breath and shaggy hair spun her around.

"No. I don't need a ride." She tried to shake his hands off, but they were like meaty vise grips, clamped down hard enough to leave bruises.

A spike of adrenaline zipped through her bloodstream as the heat of anger built. She hated being held against her will. For the past two years, she'd lived free of constraint of any kind. She'd be damned if any man would hold her back again. "Let go of me before I hurt you."

The man guffawed, spewing clouds of alcohol vapor in her face. "A little thang like you? Hurt me?"

She raised her knee in a quick jerk, connecting with the drunk's private parts.

The foul-mouthed man let go of her arms and grabbed his crotch, swearing in a high-pitched whine. "Damn, girl, I'll get ya for that."

"Yeah, right. Go home to your wife and sleep it off." She backed away and walked on, dogged by the sound of multiple footsteps in the gravel now following her. When she reached a row of cars, she stopped and wheeled around to face the new threat. "What do you want?"

The two men who looked remarkably alike and dressed identically in crisp white button-down dress shirts and neatly pressed jeans, stood in front of her, hands raised in surrender and grinning. Libby's heartbeat ratcheted up a notch as she stared at the Gray Wolf twins. The men she'd been drooling over not five minutes earlier.

"Audrey sent us out here to keep an eye on her favorite bartender," one of them said.

The other's eyes twinkled. "Seems like you can take care of yourself pretty well on your own. Ol' Pleaze won't try messing with you again."

If Libby had been wondering where all the good-looking cowboys had gone, she'd found the two most qualified. "Jackpot," she said beneath her breath.

The Gray Wolf brothers had to be the best-looking cowboys in the area, especially the twins. Their dark-skin, long, pitch-black hair and brown-black eyes spoke to their Kiowa Indian roots and had every girl this side of the Brazos River panting.

Libby had to admit, she'd panted a time or two over them from behind the bar. More and more lately. They'd made an effort to stop by and talk to her whenever she had a free moment, not that she encouraged them. It was nice on the ego to know she still had it, and appealed to a couple of damned good-looking men. Not that she could take advantage of it and flirt back. Relationships weren't in the cards for her. The twins had impeccable reputations as gentlemen and cowboys. Where women were concerned, the Gray Wolfs made fine catches.

She'd come outside for freedom from noise and people, not to start up a conversation with the cowboys. "I don't need a babysitter, but thanks anyway."

She turned and walked farther away from the building, until the thump, thump, thump of the music blaring inside the corrugated tin walls subsided some.

The crunch of boots on the gravel indicated her tail hadn't taken the hint.

"Shh!" She faced the men and pressed a finger to her lips. "Hear that?"

Both men shook their heads, the similarity between the twins so remarkable, Libby had never been able to tell them apart by looks, only by personality.

Mark, the fun-loving, more outgoing one of the pair grinned. "I don't hear a thing."

Luke shook his head. "That's her point, brother. She came out for quiet, not to hear us flapping our jaws. Come on." Luke grabbed his brother's arm. "Leave Libby alone."

"No, I'm here to watch out for the pretty lady," Mark insisted. "I don't shirk my responsibility."

"You heard her. She can take care of herself." Luke snorted. "You just wanna flirt."

"Damn right." Mark grabbed Libby's hand, swung her out and back in with his best dance move. When he had her in the crook of his arm, he whispered, "I've been trying to get inside her panties since she started here at the Ugly Stick."

Libby's pussy clenched at the thought of Mark in her panties, but she pushed the image aside and twirled out, putting distance between her and Mark. "You and every other horndog in this joint."

"Smooth, dickhead. I'm sure she goes for those kinds of come-ons." Luke reached out and captured Libby's hand. "Excuse my coarse brother, he never learned manners."

Libby laughed. Mark and Luke always had a way of lightening her dark thoughts. "You two are too much. How come you haven't found girlfriends?"

Mark grinned. "We've been waiting for you,

darlin'." He took her hand again and brought it to his lips.

Luke squeezed the fingers on her other hand gently, his gaze capturing hers, dark and intense. "We were meant for the forever kind of love, not just flirting."

Luke's words made the smile slip from Libby's lips, the hands holding hers suddenly feeling like manacles. She tugged loose and stepped back, the trapped feeling making her chest tighten, her breaths shorten and her feet itch to run.

"See there, Luke. You're scaring her now." Mark rolled his eyes. "Can't decide if the bullshit is on the inside or the outside of his boots."

Libby pulled away, fighting to breathe past the lump forming in her throat. When she spied her black and red Harley Davidson motorcycle, she hurried toward it, the road calling to her. Not until she'd swung her leg over the seat and braced her hands on the grips did she feel reason return and with it, the confirmation it was time to move on.

The twins followed, staying true to their promise to Audrey to look out for Libby.

"Beautiful." Luke smoothed his hand along the white angel wings painted across the black gas tank, but his eyes were on Libby, not the wings. "There's nothing like riding, is there?"

"Nothing," she agreed, her gaze captured by his intensely dark and sincere eyes.

These men weren't just about flirting and scoring

with every woman they met. They'd proven over and over that they were honest, helpful and kind as well. On more than one occasion, they'd lent their construction experience to Audrey and the Ugly Stick, free of charge. As Libby knew, not every handsome man had that kind of integrity. Libby had met her share of horses' asses back in New York City. She suspected the oldest of the Gray Wolf brothers, Jackson, had a lot to do with Mark and Luke's good manners, having raised them since their parents died.

"I've always imagined riding a bike is like riding a horse," Luke continued.

"It's better." Libby tipped her head back in an attempt to ignore the twinkle in his eyes. "It's like pure freedom."

"You seem to know your way around a motorcycle." Mark touched the leather seat. "Have you always been a biker?"

Libby's lips quirked and she opened her eyes. "No. Not always."

"Then why biking?" he asked.

"I go where and when I want to." Libby tipped her chin up as a light breeze lifted the hair off her neck. "No strings, no holds, just me and the road."

"That's how I feel when I'm on horseback." Luke glanced down at the bike.

"Have you ever ridden a horse?" Mark asked.

She nodded. "Lots of times."

Mark's brows rose. "Really? Around here?"

"No," she answered. "Back in New York City." As

soon as the words were out of her mouth, Libby regretted them. The less anyone knew about her former life, the better.

Mark snorted. "That's not riding, that's walking the dog. I'm talking about really riding across the range, over acres and acres, with the sun on your back and nothing around but the horse and the sky." He patted his chest. "Now that's freedom."

Libby tilted her head. She'd never seen Mark so quietly enthused. Most often he was raising a ruckus on the dance floor, twirling some pretty young thing in a short, flouncy skirt and studded cowboy boots. When he talked about riding, his face grew serious, his expression dreamy and far away.

God, he was gorgeous. Libby's tummy tightened. "No, I haven't ridden like that." But the way he talked about it made her want to.

"You should come with us," Luke said. "Why not Thursday? You're usually off on Thursday, aren't you?"

Libby frowned, not sure whether she should be annoyed or flattered that Luke knew so much about her work schedule. For certain, she didn't like the way her pulse sped at the thought of spending the day with the Gray Wolf men.

"I have…plans."

"Can't you change them?" Mark asked. "We can show you the ranch. The weather's supposed to be warm and sunny, not too hot."

The tug of the road pulled at Libby. With a man

on either side of her, she felt just a little hemmed in…
trapped. She got off her bike and stepped out of their
overpowering huddle.

"No…no, I can't change my plans." Agreeing to go
out with the men would be the biggest commitment
she'd made in the past eight months, second only to
hiring on at the Ugly Stick Saloon and becoming fast
friends with her boss.

"What plans?" Mark demanded, coming after her.

She backed up another step, her gaze going to
Luke who'd stood back, his brows dipping slightly. "I
don't know…plans." Heat rose up her neck, spreading
out into her cheeks at the lie.

"Back off, Mark. You're crowding her." Luke
grabbed his brother's arm and held him steady while
Libby stepped farther away.

Mark shook off Luke's hand and stood still,
letting the gap between himself and Libby widen.
"You like peace and quiet don't you?" he asked, his
tone softer, gentler, his eyes wide like a sad puppy's,
begging for affection. Beautiful and dangerous to her
control.

Libby couldn't resist, and nodded. "Yes."

"And she's not getting much of that now." Luke
shook his head. "Look, if you feel like getting out in
the open air, no cars, no honking, nobody to pester
you but the two of us—and I promise we won't pester
you too much—drop by our place at eleven o'clock
on Thursday. We'd love for you to join us on a ride."

Libby's eyes narrowed. The way Luke had pulled

his brother back and left the invitation open appealed to her, making her wonder what it would be like to have more of his intuitive attention, maybe even having those large, capable hands skimming across her skin, awakening places that had been long dormant. And Mark's broad shoulders and eager, brown-eyed gaze tripped her heartbeat and sent butterflies fluttering through her belly. No. She shook her head in an attempt to clear it of the vision of delicious twin cowboys. She couldn't get sucked in. She opened her mouth to decline.

Luke put up a hand. "Don't decide now. Sleep on it. You have a couple days to think about it."

"We can be as peaceful and quiet as you want," Mark promised.

Libby couldn't help her snort. "Mark...quiet? I don't think I've ever seen you quiet."

His brows furrowed. "I can be, especially out on the ranch."

She sighed. "I'll think about it."

"Great!" Mark clapped his hands together. "We'll see you at eleven on Thursday. Wear boots and jeans. We'll make it a picnic."

Libby chuckled. "I said I'd think about it."

"Libby!" Audrey's voice carried across the back parking lot.

"We'll be countin' the minutes until we see you again." Luke captured her hand and lifted it to his lips.

Libby's cheeks warmed and a deep yearning low

in her belly blossomed, making her ache for more than just a kiss on her hand.

"The two of us will make it a treat you won't forget," Mark promised, sweeping her into a bear hug, lifting her off the ground and planting a kiss on her surprised lips. Before she could find her wits to struggle, he set her back on her feet and tucked something in her jeans' pocket. "If you need us for anything..." He waggled his eyebrows. "And I mean anything...call." He spun her toward the building and patted her bottom.

Libby hurried back into the saloon, wondering what had just happened. She pulled a card from her hip pocket and stared down at the logo for Gray Wolf Architectural Designs and the phone number listed.

"Oh good, I was beginning to think the twins had absconded with my best bartender." Audrey leaned closer, her eyes narrowing. "Are you all right?"

Libby jammed the card back into her pocket, frowning. "I think I'm going on a picnic."

Audrey laughed. "Did Mark and Luke talk you into an outing?" She patted Libby on the back. "Babe, you're in for a real treat."

"That's what *they* said." A tingle of excitement threatened to grow inside Libby's body.

A secret smile lifted Audrey's lips. "The two of them are amazing together."

Her frown deepening, Libby glanced across at her boss. "And you know that *how*?"

Audrey's lips quirked upward in a smirk. "Did I

tell you the story of how they got me and Jackson together?" She slipped her arm around Libby's shoulder and walked her slowly into the bar.

"No, you didn't."

Audrey touched a finger to her own lips. "Hmm. Maybe I shouldn't, and let you discover for yourself why those two are phenomenal."

Libby's core tightened, a wash of moisture trickling out of what she'd thought was her dried-up pussy, shocking her more than she cared to admit. She marched the rest of the way to the bar and took up her bar towel. "I've a good mind to cancel."

"No way," Audrey called out.

Her heart sped and pressure pushed against her chest, the sure signs of the beginnings of an anxiety attack.

Audrey laid a hand on her arm. "You have to go on that picnic. I promise you won't regret it."

Forcing a smile for the next customer, Libby muttered beneath her breath, "I think I already am." *Yeah, yeah.* Then why did a shiver of anticipation spread throughout her body?

ABOUT MYLA JACKSON AKA ELLE JAMES

Twenty years of livin' and lovin' on a South Texas ranch raising horses, cattle, ostriches and emus left an indelible impression on Myla Jackson, one she likes to instill in her red-hot stories. Myla pens wildly sexy, fun adventures of all genres including historical westerns, medieval, romantic suspense, contemporary and paranormal beasties of all shapes and sexy sizes. When she's not wrangling words from her computer she's traveling, boating, riding her ATV or spending time with family. She lives in the tree-covered hills of Northwest Arkansas with her husband and her muses—human-wanna-be canines —Chewy and Sweetpea.

To learn more about Myla Jackson and Elle James visit her website at www.mylajackson.com

mylajackson.com
mylajackson@mylajackson.com